FLESH EATERS

A Novella   99¢

Alisha Adkins

FLESH EATERS

by Alisha Adkins

Table of Contents

Dedication

In memory of Elvis, my beloved companion of eighteen years. He was my one constant through an otherwise tumultuous, ever-changing life—seeing me through college, several careers, two marriages, one divorce, Hurricane Katrina, and moving fifteen times. My beautiful, perfect boy—every night he slept on my pillow beside my head, tucking his paws in my hand and resting his head on top of it. I spent more of my life with him than any single human being, and I was perpetually astonished that, even after so many years, each day I was filled with new delight at seeing him. I will always be grateful for our years together and deeply feel his absence. I loved him totally and unreservedly, with all my heart, and I always will.

Part 1: London Calls

"The ice age is coming,

the sun is zooming in.

Engines stop running,

and the wheat is growing thin.

A nuclear era,

but I have no fear.

London is drowning,

and I live by the river."

—London Calling, The Clash

Chapter 1

As I awoke, I hazily noticed that my face was pressed against hard, cool cement. It wasn't gravelly sidewalk cement, but vaguely shiny, almost lacquered cement like one commonly finds in college dormitories and other clinical institutions. Although I wasn't accustomed to waking up on hard surfaces, I was willing to ignore it for the moment and flutter in and out of consciousness for a while. Unfortunately, I wasn't allowed the luxury of easing into consciousness, as I like to do after sleeping, for, as my eyes focused, I was compelled to jolt up.

I was immediately, painfully, alert; a large, muscular man was standing over me. I couldn't help thinking about how closely he resembled the brutish archetype I'd seen in so many video games. His chest was disproportionately large, and his bulbous arms sprouted out of his faded T-shirt, contributing to his polygonal appearance. His hands were oversized, even for his frame, and looked blocky. His taut, angular face stared down at me.

The large man hovering over me was aiming what appeared to be an equally large revolver at my head. I focused my attention there, staring into the depths of the barrel, bewildered. He was saying something, but my adrenaline was pumping, and the sound of my heart was deafening. Aware that this was a classic "fight or flight" situation, I bitterly began to wonder what was keeping me from choosing a response. I seemed frozen, or perhaps time had stood still.

There was someone else, behind him, shouting; this figure was a blur to me—a blue blur (his shirt, I think) with a shiny, metallic tracer. The blur's words "Shoot her! Shoot her!" seemed to make their way through the cyclone of movement and confusion.

My trance was broken. Facing the absurd realization that my death was imminent, I sprang awake. I frantically looked around me, desperate for something, anything. A nearby exit caught my attention; a few yards from me, there was a dark hole at the bottom of the wall. The hole was close to two feet tall and appeared either to be an air vent or, perhaps, my reeling mind postulated, a drainage duct leading to sewers. I began to start for it, but jerked myself to a stop before I had even begun to move, quickly seeing that it was futile. The hole was blocked off; across the opening hung what looked like it would prove to be a very heavy latticed, metal grate.

I started to turn away in search of some other means of escape, but caught a glimpse of something odd from the corner of my eye. Looking again, I noticed that a handgun sat near the grate. There was a shotgun a few feet beyond that.

I didn't stop to look a gift gun in the mouth. Somewhere deep in the recesses of my churning psyche, I was whispering reassuringly to myself. In a soothing voice, I told myself that I didn't need to (or have time to) question why I had woken up in this strange, new environ, let alone why there was a stockpile of guns lying a few yards from me. I tried to reach for the handgun, but my progress was impeded.

To this day, I still can't work out all of the details of those first few minutes after I woke up; everything was happening too fast. My adversaries' shouting mixed with my own, bleeding together into a thunderous, unintelligible hum. Their movements seemed to meld them into one giant, nebulous enemy. Straining for the revolver, I felt as though I were fumbling for a light switch in the dark. I remember thinking that my burly assailant must be sitting on my chest; I'm still not sure if he was, or if my lower half had failed to wake up with the rest of me. Whatever was holding me back, I lay prone and, stretching and contorting, finally managed to wriggle away from the two men, just far enough to grasp the gun.

I had no idea if the thing was loaded, but since I'd heard a hammer being cocked amidst the cacophony, I knew it was my only hope. The blue blur was rushing at me, looking more and more like a skinny, unkempt man with a gun as he did so. I raised the gun and fired.

I am not a gun person. I have had no formal training with guns. In fact, the only time my father took me shooting, the sound of the guns firing made me cover my ears with my hands and cry to be taken home. I would have been lucky to hit my blurry blue attacker at all. That I shot him in the forehead with what to a casual observer would have only looked like dead accuracy is another baffling detail in the bizarre, surrealistic world I had fallen into.

I had no time to breathe a sigh of relief, as the second gunman was bearing down on me, uttering nasty guttural noises. That he hadn't shot me yet was inexplicable to me at the time. In retrospect, I attribute it to the crazed way I had been shaking my head around. Since I had not actually faced a situation remotely like this before, it seemed perfectly appropriate to me to hysterically thrash my head about. I believe my spasmodic behavior saved my life. I'm sure he was holding out for a clean shot; he needed to conserve ammo.

I managed to stagger to my feet. He was only a foot or two away from me now and was trying to grab my arms, to hold me still.

I raised the gun toward him, levying it to what I presumed was his chest level. I wasn't even looking at what I was doing. I could only look at him—and his gun. His gun was shiny and black, and I would have sworn it was the size of a cannon. He was still trying to get a good hold on me, to get a clear shot at my head.

I fired. He staggered back; a blood spot materialized on the upper chest area of his shirt, instantly plastering the cloth to his chest, and began to spread outwards. He swayed and then lumbered forward for me again. I shot him again. I didn't even hear the gun shots as I unloaded them. I knew I'd fired when he fell backwards. His heavy frame hit the floor solidly, resonating. Blood emptied out of him and pooled around his body.

The echo of his fall began to fade, and was replaced with momentary stillness. I stood up and inhaled deeply.

Then the bullet-ridden oaf leaped up and lunged at me. His eyes were milky and dead.

I was vaguely aware that my feet had involuntarily begun to shuffle backwards; I remember hearing the soles of my boots scuffing against the cement below me.

I felt as though I'd walked into a zombie movie. The reassuring whisper that resided inside of me promptly gave up and went silent. Still, I had no time to be incredulous; he had hold of me. I accepted that I was living in an obscure, low-budget movie and resolved to deal with my complete and utter loss of sanity after I had disposed of my undead assailant. He had dropped his gun after the second shot I fired into him. It lay in his blood, forgotten. This hulking abomination was more concerned with immediate gratification now. He was looming over me, grabbing at my arms, digging his nails into me. His mouth was descending toward my shoulder, gaping hungrily.

Face to face with what bore more than a passing resemblance to a hungry zombie, I did what any self-respecting horror buff would. I shot for the head. At point blank range, he really didn't have a chance.

The monstrosity roared and seemed to fall back in slow motion. His limbs twitched wildly. Then everything went silent.

Dumbstruck, I stood, motionless, staring down at his body. Anyone who's ever seen a horror flick knows you should never stand within arm's reach of your fallen adversary. But I lingered there, inches from him. For hours? For days? Maybe it was only minutes. All sense of time deserted me that day (nor have I ever fully regained it since).

The bullet wound in his head couldn't have been more than a dime in size; it was deep and dark, but bloodless. The skin around the wound was loose and turgid, pushed into unnatural ridges. Staring blankly down at the carcass, I found myself thinking that his forehead resembled a mountain range with the abscess, a valley in its middle. Then I began to think that his forehead looked more like an enormous shortbread cookie with a dollop of dark raspberry filling at its center. This analogy disturbed me, and I forced myself to look away.

I surveyed the room. It was small, dimly lit with covered, fluorescent lighting, and made of cement, painted off-white. Just beyond the corpse, there was a drain in the middle of the slightly concave cement floor.

The drain was currently being put to work; a stream of blood was winding a meandering path into it, emptying in a slow but steady drip. My assailant had recklessly trekked his own vital fluids around him, daubing the floor with his juices during his repeated, frantic attempts to assault me. In addition to the substantial puddle he had left near the middle of the room, streaks and droplets blanketed the chamber.

The grated hole and shotgun lay behind me to my left. I began to think about what chance I might have of ever wrenching the damned grate off and where the opening might lead. I was not hopeful on either count. The more frail of my two antagonists lay near this duct. Taking a few steps closer, I was able to get a better look at him.

He was lying face up. The bullet wound was hard to miss. If the wound in his forehead was larger than his friend's, it was imperceptibly so. However, long trails of blood had run, in rivulets, down all sides of his face, pooling around his chin and in his ears. Avoiding looking at his eyes, I gingerly grasped a tuft of his ratty hair and lifted his head. The back half of his skull was almost entirely gone. His head looked like a broken hard-boiled egg out of which someone had plucked the yolk. Then I began to notice the bits of gore strewn about him that were presumably scraps of brain matter.

Abruptly dropping his head, I stifled a gag and turned back around.

Where the hell was I?

Turning, I looked to my right. The room in which I found myself appeared to be a very large shower room. This hypothesis was strongly corroborated by the fact that there was an ornate-looking shower head on the opposite wall. There was also a door—a fairly standard, run-of-the-mill opaque glass door. How could I have missed it before? Feeling suddenly decidedly less restrained, I walked over to it. My boots made unpleasant squishing noises in the wetness below me.

The door was slightly ajar; bright light poured through the crack. I cautiously peered into the adjoining room. It was a bathroom. More importantly, it appeared to be empty. I slid the door open.

The bathroom was immaculate. It was brilliantly white: the walls were ivory with alabaster molding, and the sink faucet and porcelain commode gleamed. The mirror above the sink reflected the overhead light, making the room's illumination almost blinding. It looked totally unlived in; there was no rug on the floor, no toothbrush on the sink counter—not a single sign of use. It looked like a mock-up bathroom in a department store.

I entered the virginal room, tracking blood across the floor as I went. Stopping in front of the mirror, I ventured a look at myself. My left cheek was streaked with blood. My hair was knotted and caked with foul stickiness; strands clung to my face. I was wearing an army-green T-shirt, spackled with blood, and loose-fitting grey-black jeans, which also bore some nasty, darker smears. I had had some vain hope that seeing what I was wearing would jog my memory. I thought I might remember where I had been when I put my clothes on, or what I had been doing—some event that might have led me here. No memory came. They were my clothes, but they offered me no recollection of how I had gotten here.

I set the gun down on the sink counter and washed my face. After spending a few moments fruitlessly trying to pick coagulated blood from my matted hair, I gave up in disgust. Even though the room gave off the impression that no human had ever set foot in it before, I figured that I had best search it, just to be thorough. I didn't want to miss even the smallest clue that might lend me a wisp of insight into where I was or what was going on. Besides, I'd played enough Resident Evil to know that, during a zombie outbreak, protagonists were supposed to pilfer any supplies they could find. I rifled through the drawers below the counter. The first drawer produced a bottle containing two aspirin, an empty tube of toothpaste, and a pen cap. I pocketed the aspirin. The second drawer appeared empty, but careful examination led to what I considered an exciting discovery. In the back corner lay a small, brown band—a hair tie.

Shutting the drawers, I quickly gathered up my fetid hair and bound it into a ponytail. Feeling moderately refreshed, I retrieved the gun from the counter and turned to the door on my right—the door that led out into the rest of the apartment, if where I found myself was indeed an apartment.

Chapter 2

The door opened into a sterile, white hallway. Tentatively creeping along the corridor, I noticed an intercom mounted into the wall. Beside it stood a solid door, made of thick wood, possessing a small peephole.

Presuming that this was the entrance to the residence I found myself in, I looked through the hole. I could see very little, but what I could see didn't look very inviting—a few feet of wall, stained with brown blotches and dribbles. I abandoned the door, continuing down the hallway.

The hallway led into a pristine kitchen. The counter tops were spotless and barren, save for a small microwave. It was a typical kitchen, containing a refrigerator-freezer, a stove with an oven, a dishwasher-type appliance, a built-in washer-dryer (odd, I thought), and an extensive counter with numerous cabinets above and below it. Opening the cabinets, I found them all to be empty.

There was an architectural oddity to this room; its one "window" was not a traditional window, but a screened, triangular opening. The wide bottom of the opening began above the stove and it tapered up, its tip ending at the ceiling. Being just a tad over five feet tall, I had to stand back from the aperture and on tiptoes to look through it. There appeared to be an empty space directly beyond the window and another brightly lit, sterile-looking apartment was visible through an identical "window" several yards away. It seemed that this apartment was probably part of some sort of complex with a courtyard in the middle. I stood for a while, watching, but was unable to detect any signs of movement in the residence across from me.

The apartment's emptiness felt ominous, and its silence was overbearing; I had the eerie sense that I was traversing an inordinately posh tomb. What was this antiseptic place? Why were its only inhabitants zombies? And how the hell did I get here, anyway? Through what mysterious wormhole in the time-space continuum must I have passed in order to wind up stranded in this god-forsaken, post-apocalyptic, *I Am Legend* world?

I left the kitchen. The living room was tasteful, but something about it seemed wrong. There was a large, plush sofa in the middle of the room, facing a large television on a stand. A small table stood to one side of the couch; a phone rested on it. It was the kind of living room anybody would find acceptable; it had everything a living room requires. Still, it felt sparse. There were no real signs of habitation—no knickknacks, no mementos, no books or magazines—no personal possessions.

The lights were dim here, and the television was on, casting flickering images across the sofa. The broadcast was merely noiseless snow. I found the remote on the sofa and hunted for a station that might still be coming in. My heart sank further with every channel I flipped. Finally, I switched to a channel with a coherent picture. My heart leaped up into my throat, beating fast. My excitement was wasted, however. The screen merely contained wavering text, passively advising me to "please stand by."

The telephone was equally unproductive. I picked it up, though clueless as to whom I should dial if it happened to work. A persistent beeping busy signal greeted me, periodically interrupted by a recorded message. In a female voice with a very proper-sounding British accent, the message informed me that systems in my area were currently out of order and that I should try my call again later. The beeps and message repeated again... and again... I hung up the phone.

Indifferent, I noted that my predicament appeared to not be so isolated. The whole city (what city was this? Could it be London? How could I have wound up in Britain?) seemed to be experiencing some difficulties. I reasoned that a zombie problem, if there was indeed such a thing, would have to be fairly widespread to put a city—or perhaps even a whole metropolitan area—out of service. Sitting on the lush sofa in the darkness of the living room, I stared vacantly down at my right foot. I probably looked at the eyelet of my boot for ten full minutes. My mind was blissfully blank. I eventually noticed that my shoelaces were untied. Morsels of gore had been ground into one of the laces. My eyes traveled down to the sole. Blood was caked into the treads, up over the sides of the sole and onto the lower boot. I vaguely wondered if it was possible to get blood out of leather.

I remained numb for a long time. Eventually, sitting in the gloom, gazing at my shoe, sensations began to return. Since the attack, some regulatory system within my body had seen fit to shut my emotions off and let me fly on automatic pilot. Perhaps my body knew it would function more competently without erroneous emotions muddling things, or perhaps it was trying to conserve my sensibilities until my environment was sane enough to support them. Either way, my dulled thoughts and feelings were starting to reemerge, and I couldn't say that I welcomed them. Actually, I resented their return; I wanted to remain detached—it kept me insulated. Now panic was beginning to well up inside of me. I told myself to keep moving.

I bent down and tied my shoelaces. Then, gun in hand, I proceeded to explore. I resolved to make certain that the entire apartment was clear; then, I told myself, I would be safe. Then I could think. It made me feel better, to have a purpose. It was something upon which to focus.

I followed the hallway that adjoined the living room. A door hung open to my right; glancing in furtively, I saw that it was a bedroom, empty except for an elaborately canopied queen-size bed. I skipped the door to the left for the moment and approached the door at the end of the hallway. I reached for the doorknob and attempted to turn it, but it resisted. A locked door? I wasn't sure what that meant. But my purpose was to make this place my safe haven, at least until I had some grasp of what was going on, so I was determined to open the door.

Taking a deep breath and a few steps back, I ran at the door, ramming it with my shoulder. The door shuddered under the force, but didn't give way. My newly bruised shoulder smarted quite a lot. The wood seemed to be fairly flimsy, so I rested for a minute, took a few more deep breaths, and then launched into it again. This time the door shattered along its frame; I tumbled onto a bathroom floor amidst a shower of sharp wood splints.

I had begun to doubt what I had seen earlier, thinking that, in my terror, my imagination had conjured up the farcical notion that a zombie was after me. After all, in times of stress, the mind can play morbid pranks. Had my mind invented the dead look in that brawny man's eyes?

What stood over me now dispelled any doubts I had. The thing hovering over me had definitely been dead for a long time. It was female (or at least once had been), and she was putrid. Even before I saw her, her foul odor hit me. The rankness was overpowering; there's really nothing I could liken it to aside from the stench of a ripe animal carcass, teeming with diverse populations of larvae, that has been left to fester in the sun for a few weeks. Which is pretty much what she was. She seemed to have festered right here though, if the décor of the room was any indication; foul smudges adorned the walls around her.

She shrieked, though where the sound came from I couldn't say, since her throat looked like it was in pretty sorry shape. Then she pounced upon me. I wrestled with her, gagging. Her flesh was slimy and slid off in filmy sheets, adhering to my fingers as I attempted to restrain her arms. What she lacked in strength, she made up for in sheer vileness. When she lowered her head to take a chunk out of my cheek, my head reeled from the smell her open mouth emitted. As her head lingered over mine, droplets of unidentifiable brownish fluid oozed from her, pelting my cheek.

I seized her by her face and flung her off of me. I scrambled up; she was picking herself up off of the floor. Quickly, I raised the gun and fired. Her head virtually exploded, raining moist black chunks of filth over me and across the floor.

I bent over and retched for a while. Then I stepped over her headless remains and washed the muck from my hands and face. Holding my hand over my nose and mouth, I inspected the room as quickly as possible. The body was clothed in a badly stained and rather frilly dress. It was hard to tell, but it looked as though she had died from a leg wound. Although rotten, she was mostly intact except for one of her legs, where a good portion was jaggedly wrenched away, as if by persistent teeth, and the bone was exposed.

The corpse I spied in the corner corroborated this hypothesis. It was even less fresh than was the girl, and its skull had been shattered by a bullet. An abandoned gun lay nearby. Conjuring an explanation, I imagined that the girl had been attacked, and though she had killed the undead invader, the fiend had badly wounded her during the scuffle. She then locked herself in, hoping to thwart the urges she knew that she would develop, and waited to die. Somehow, it made me feel better to give my revolting, yet pathetic, assailant a story, however fantastical. An explanation, *any* explanation, at least provided structure, a set of bizarre game rules, so to speak, for this psychotic fantasy role-play world I was now unwillingly exploring.

Looking around me, I noted that there was a connecting room; it was a smaller version of the other cement shower room I had encountered, and it was empty. Having done a perfunctory, but adequate, inspection of the area, I quickly took my leave of the bathroom.

Stepping back into the hallway, I slumped against the wall and breathed, sucking in greedily, having found a new appreciation for even relatively fresh air.

Chapter 3

I felt strong. Whatever horrors lurked here, I knew I would beat them. This apartment was *mine*. I couldn't speculate on what insanity was occurring in the world outside, what atrocities might be being committed, but here I would be master. I was in control. I was safe. I was invincible.

Even as I was bolstering my confidence though, a question began to nag at me, needling its way into the forefront of my thoughts. I had a terrible, sinking feeling. It would be just terrific to secure this lavish apartment and hide out here while zombies roamed the world outside. Just swell. But I'd forgotten one minor detail. How the hell was I going to feed myself? Even if the refrigerator were well stocked, an unlikely scenario in this lifeless imposter of an apartment, how long could that food last? How long would the electricity even continue to run?

Eventually, I was going to have to go foraging. But if zombies were busy munching the street merchants, what then? Where, exactly, would I procure food? No one was going to deliver pizza during a zombie infestation! Would the farmers, if any had survived, choose to dodge the zombies in their fields in order to harvest their crops? No, they would probably be otherwise occupied. So, with all of humanity presumably fleeing the undead plague, who was left to produce? We were all very good at consuming, but would *anyone* produce?

That's when I began wondering whether one could eat zombies. I knew it was an insane idea to mull over, but I toyed with it none the less. It was a personal joke, really—a mental exercise intended to keep me busy. Of course, I wouldn't consider eating a decayed, odorous corpse like the girl in the bathroom. The bacteria would kill me. But what about a fresher specimen, one recently deceased? If I were to eat a zombie, it would have to be someone who died and then was put to rest a second time very shortly thereafter. Much like my muscular friend from earlier, I realized. He hadn't been a zombie all along, had he? No, he had only gotten that unpleasant, I'm-going-to-eat-your-flesh demeanor after I had shot him a few times. And his friend... he never turned at all. I shot him in the head the first time. He never got the chance to reanimate.

So, those two were perfect examples. They would be fresh enough to consume. But if one were to eat a zombie, would that turn one into a zombie?

I had only begun to muse over this question when things seemed to start to click in my mind. If those two thugs hadn't been zombies all along, why did they want to kill me? It might sound a bit vain, but I don't think I bore even the slightest resemblance to a walking corpse. Then I thought of how the oaf ("Bluto," as I dubbed him for my own amusement) had kept trying to hold my head still, for a clean shot. If he shot me in the head the first time, I would never get the chance to reanimate. My disturbing hypothesis was this: he knew I was human, but whether I was human or not, he was hungry. He was preparing a meal.

"Well, that's far-fetched, not to mention highly paranoid," I said aloud. Telling myself that I was delusional made me feel oddly better, and the added touch of talking to myself helped reaffirm my obvious instability. Having successfully cut off that line of thinking, I propelled myself into action again, approaching the final unexplored room.

Chapter 4

I slowly pushed the door open, gun readied. Nothing leaped at me. I stepped inside. It was another bedroom, but it was different from the first. Really, it was different from every other room in the residence; it looked like someone lived there. There were chests of drawers, a nightstand, a desk with a computer sitting atop it (a screen saver was still running), a poster of a nondescript boy band, and two twin-size beds. One of the beds wasn't even made! The covers were rumpled and bunched up in places, and a corner dangled off of the edge. I sat down on the disheveled bed, feeling a bit like Goldilocks.

I sat peacefully, making a conscientious effort to relax. A rustling noise made me jump. The room was silent again for a moment. Then there was a bump… then a scraping sound. It was coming from the closet.

The closet door was ajar; I eased it open with my foot, gun raised. Behind the thick foliage of coats and sweaters, something was moving.

"Come out! Slowly!" I bid the rustling figure. After what I'd seen that day, I knew it was naïve to bark orders at what was surely another festering automaton, but I did it anyway.

A feeble shape gradually emerged from the clothing. It was a boy; he was unnaturally thin, with an ashen complexion.

I couldn't ascertain if he was alive or dead.

I held the gun against his head. His eyes were wide and watery. He outstretched his skeletal arms.

"Keep back!" I commanded, although the gesture seemed pathetic; it resembled a pleading act more than an overt threat.

"Can you speak?" I asked, retaining my firm tone.

"Ye… ye… yess…" he spluttered, nodding his head emphatically. "Yes, Miss."

His upturned face, sallow and frightened, looked at me imploringly.

"You're alive?" I was skeptical. His appearance fell right on the cusp; he could have been sickly and near death, or he could have recently perished. There was no rulebook I could consult to concretely determine if all zombies were unable to speak. Sure, in movies the occasional groan was the most dialogue you could hope for from one, but since when did movies get anything right?

"Yes! Yes, I'm alive." He was adamant.

"Well, let's just prove that theory, shall we?" I retorted.

I grasped him by his arm and led him over to the poster on the wall. There, I dropped his arm and told him to stay put. With the gun still trained on him, I used my left hand to dislodge a tack from the heartthrobs' portrait. Taking hold of his slender little arm once more, I used the tack to carve a deep furrow in his forearm. Blood seeped to the surface. The boy was biting his lip, stifling a sob.

I was convinced. The dead don't bleed.

Cutting a helpless child was probably the most despicable act I'd performed yet, but I made no apologies. I released his wounded arm, murmuring, "Alright." I wanted to tousle his fine blonde hair and reassure him, but I couldn't. I had no social text to follow, and I felt tired and awkward, almost paralyzed.

The boy was far from paralyzed; words poured out of him, flavored by his English schoolboy speech.

"It's so good to see someone who's alive again, Miss. Mum and Dad went for help weeks ago. I've been hiding for so long... I'm Timmy," he added, extending his hand. Vacantly, I shook it.

"Adrienne," I said.

"Pleased to meet you," Timmy said. His politeness struck me as exorbitant, under the circumstances.

I had many questions to ask, but I couldn't organize them in my head. Meanwhile, Timmy continued to spout. I sat back on the bed and listened.

He told me that he was nine years old and that he and his family had lived in the flat we were in for as long as he could remember. He said that the "monsters" had come well over a month ago.

"I was out with my mum shopping; my birthday was coming up, and she was going to get me a new game for my PlayStation 2. Anyway, as we were walking, we started noticing people were being catcn... right there on the street. So mum took my hand, and we started running..."

He told me that they had fled back to the flat, and there the family had waited for the problem to end. But it didn't end. The armed forces had been dispatched, but were quickly defeated; the massacred soldiers only bolstered the numbers of dead with which citizens had to contend. Warnings came, urging everyone to evacuate. His family, along with most of the other residents in their building, remained holed up in their apartments. Their contact with other people, including friends and family, was severed. Occasionally, they would heard their neighbors tossing zombies out of their windows into the courtyard, which had quickly become a repository for the undead and other refuse. Eventually, they didn't hear anything anymore. Then the news reports stopped. The world outside seemed to go silent.

"That was when Mum and Dad said that they would go for help. They said they'd come back for us as soon as they found somewhere safe for us all. So, we helped them pack up everything they would need for the trip, and then we locked ourselves in when they left. Constance and I stayed in our bedroom for the first few days, but then we started hearing noises. Constance said she'd stand guard with the gun... I hid in the closet. I've been in the closet for a while."

From his pasty complexion, I could tell that he had.

A few carefully tailored questions elicited enough information about his sister for me to ascertain that the headless heap in the bathroom was Constance, but I didn't have the heart to tell him.

Nor did I have the heart to tell Timmy that if his parents had really intended to return and escort the children to safety, they probably would not have bothered to take everything except the bulky furniture they could not move. They hadn't left their children with any amenities—not even toothpaste, or plates, or cups, or utensils. They'd taken every last item that had even a trace of value or personal meaning. It didn't seem to me that Mom and Dad were planning to return. It seemed to me that Mom and Dad had run for their lives, and discarded the belongings that would slow them down, which apparently included their children. Little Timmy and Constance were merely cumbersome, unfortunate detriments, hindrances to their survival.

I swallowed my disgust and asked Timmy how he and his family had managed to eat.

"We had food for a while. When it ran out, we started to get really hungry. We couldn't go out; the monsters were everywhere, you know. We could hear them bumping into the walls in the hallway outside the flat some nights. Eventually, Dad said

43

something had to be done. We ate old Mrs. Dibley, from downstairs. She was the first one."

"You ate your elderly neighbor?"

"Well, she was dead. Dad said he couldn't tell if the zombies had gotten her or if her heart had given out. But she was definitely dead. Constance and I were watching from the doorway. Mrs. Dibley's eyes were scary, and she was trying to eat Dad, only she didn't have her teeth in."

"So your father shot her in the head, and the family ate her," I summarized icily.

"No. We didn't have the guns then. The Americans brought them when they came."

"Americans?"

"Yeah, the American refugees. They came after a few weeks. The states were in worse shape, Dad said. So the Americans came here to escape their dead."

"Give us your tired, your poor…" I thought. "Migrating in search of a better life…" I muttered, bitterly savoring the irony of the "superpower" nation of immigrants fearfully emigrating home to their colonial parent.

Timmy looked at me blankly.

I abandoned the mental digression. "So, how did you kill the zombies without guns?" I inquired. "Don't you have to penetrate their skulls to stop them?"

Nodding, Timmy explained, "Dad used a cricket bat."

Chapter 5

Timmy hadn't eaten since his parents had left. He was really a frail shadow of a boy; he looked like a callous artist's emaciated interpretation of a child. I needed to feed him.

Together, we went to the kitchen. The bloodstained freezer was empty. I hesitantly recounted the experience I had had with the two gunmen in the shower room. Eagerly, Timmy led me back to the scene. It was exactly as I had left it, though much of the blood had dried. Timmy pronounced them both still quite fresh so, together, we disrobed the two departed gentlemen. Timmy found a hunting knife on the body of the larger one, and busily set to work quartering them. He was quite adept at butchery, easily cleaving the muscle cleanly from the bone. He told me his parents had taught him. I tried my best to hide my queasiness.

The sight of that cherub hacking up two grown men left me more than a little unsettled.

He asked me for assistance when he came to tasks that were particularly difficult for him—tasks that required more strength than his nine-year-old frame could provide, such as sawing through bone. Under his direction, I did what was required, chanting a this-isn't-happening mantra to myself as I worked.

When we were done divesting the two of all edible flesh, and had divided them into manageable pieces, we wrapped them in strips of their clothing in lieu of butcher paper. Timmy carted them to the freezer, and when the freezer was filled, we put the remaining parcels in the refrigerator.

I put the byproducts in pillowcases I took from the children's bedroom. There were a lot of byproducts; there were bones, ligaments, and gristle, long strings of intestine, and various unidentifiable bits (innards of some sort)—and the heads, sans their tongues. Undoubtedly, we were

47

wasteful with the organs, leaving behind potentially digestible, though revolting, pieces.

I loaded up the pillowcases and lugged them through the house, leaving a grisly trail across the tiled kitchen floor as I dragged the sacks of human refuse behind me. I deposited them in the bathroom Constance was resting in, tugged the battered door solidly into its frame, and told Timmy not to go in there. He didn't ask any questions, but I think he suspected his sister was in there. He never asked me anything about her, but I could tell that he knew she was dead.

While Timmy cooked himself a meal, I collected all the guns from around the house. There were two handguns, excluding the one I was toting, and a shotgun. Unfortunately, our ammunition supply looked rather meager. I placed our arsenal on the kitchen counter and returned to the shower room. There, I scrubbed, using one of our prey's spare socks. I scrubbed until I had loosened every last chunk and then watched all of the carnage rinse away down the drain.

Timmy was eating when I returned to the kitchen. I knew he needed to; I told myself that he was weak and needed to regain his health. Still, I couldn't watch.

Chapter 6

Initially, I took an escapist approach; I pretended the cannibalism wasn't occurring and found other things to do when Timmy ate. For what I at least perceived as days, I stubbornly suffered the hunger, internally marveling at my stoicism and touting my own virtue. But I grew tired of admiring my valor, and I grew hungry. Lacking a martyr's constitution and weak from hunger, I began to rationalize that my death from starvation would do little to assay the world's problems. Following a lengthy and heated inner dispute, I caved. When I asked Timmy to make an extra portion for me, he just nodded. Timmy had a knack for knowing when it was best not to talk about things. That first meal, I just picked at my helping, pulling off strands of the striated muscle and eating them piecemeal. It took me ages to choke down an ounce or two.

Timmy considerately tried to distract me from the task at hand, a tradition he carried on at mealtime thereafter. He took the opportunity to ply me with questions.

"What did you do, when you lived in America?"

"I didn't do *anything*, really. I was a graduate student." I ate a small strip of meat, wincing.

"What did you study?"

"History primarily—that's what my bachelors degree is in—but my graduate program was more inter-disciplinary. I studied a variety of social sciences—sociology, economics, political science—all of which are utterly useless now, what with the downfall of society and all. Nothing's left to apply it to."

Brushing aside my fatalism, he continued his questions. "What were you going to do when you finished?" he inquired.

"I really don't know. It was kind of a stream-of-consciousness degree. I took what interested me at the time and figured I'd work out what to do with it down the line." I swallowed a particularly gristle-laden morsel, gulping hard.

"What do you mean, 'stream of consciousness?'" he asked.

I clarified, "One thing flowing into another... Like now."

He nodded. "You didn't want to teach, maybe?"

"Oh, god, no!" I exclaimed, momentarily almost unaware of the tidbit of meat I was trying to consume. "I could always have resorted to that, but it certainly wasn't a desirable outcome to my education!" Memories of the horrors of high school outweighed even the gravity of ingesting human flesh for a fleeting moment.

And thus went our conversation. Timmy had an instinctual flair for diverting my attention in unpleasant situations; before I knew it, the meal would be mercifully finished.

Still, knowing I had committed such a ghoulish act gnawed at me. I decided I had probably gone mad. Yes, that was the simplest answer. What was that principle? Occam's Razor, I think. The simplest answer is probably the correct one. Being insane was certainly the simplest answer. In fact, it was the only logical one. I didn't tell Timmy about the conclusion I had reached. I figured it was a moot point, since Timmy might be figment of my imagination anyway.

In all honesty, I had doubts about my insanity; I really had a feeling that I was a sane person and the rest of the world was loopy. All the same, the concrete decision that I was certifiably bonkers gave me closure; it was an explanation that made sense and freed me from a lot of pressure. I still revert back to it periodically; it's a wonderful crutch when explanations are scarce, and it excuses one from all manner of taboo behavior.

My palate acclimated rapidly. I soon ceased to look upon the food as a person and began to appreciate it as sustenance. I had shunned red meat prior to this zombie fiasco, but I began to develop a taste for it, appreciating the subtle nuances of different cuts. The meat tended to be rather tough, which I attributed mostly to lack of marinade and reliance upon microwave cooking. Timmy and I began to tenderize the meat and to use the broiler, which made the meals much more pleasurable.

A new discomfort rose up to replace my squeamishness. Although it seemed like an enormous quantity of meat, it steadily dwindled. I wondered what we would do when it was gone each time I opened the freezer. It was another topic of which Timmy seemed to know it was best not to speak, and I appreciated the temporary reprieve that his silence afforded me.

Chapter 7

When I had first seen Timmy, he had immediately brought to mind a Charles Dickens novel. It didn't make a difference which Dickens novel (particularly since I had never gotten more than a third of the way through any given Dickens novel before resorting to the Cliff's Notes)—he just had that pathetic, bedraggled English boy look. His appearance was deceptive though. He was remarkably resilient. Perhaps because of his youth, he was able to accept and adapt to these extraordinary conditions much more adeptly than could I.

Timmy and I grew close quickly. We spent our days joking, alternating between playing games on his PlayStation 2 and his computer (he always seemed to win), and generally slacking off. I felt like a big sister and was deeply protective. At nights, I'd put my arm around him and watch him go to sleep. My own sleep was fitful at best.

Some nights I'd stay up all night and watch him. When I did sleep, my dreams were plagued with zombies—usually defiled loved ones from my half-forgotten life in the U.S. The dreams haunted me; they were more ghastly even than reality. My subconscious was unconscionably cruel, tainting the few pleasant memories I still retained. Everything I had, all of my emotional energy, I put into Timmy instead, resolving not to look back or wonder what had happened to the people I had loved in that previous life.

Time passed quickly. All of our days were alike and ran together; each day, we ate, and talked, and played, and slept, and tried not to dream. It's amazing how quickly one can adapt a new routine and make a lifestyle one's own. It felt as though we had always lived in that apartment, he and I, with nothing but time to while away on frivolous conversation and mind-numbing computer games. It was strangely comfortable. The world outside remained silent and was thus easy to ignore. It existed only in the very back of our minds.

When Timmy and I had first started to talk to one another, I tried to edit my speech, choosing my words carefully in an attempt to gloss over delicate subject matter.

However, I soon realized that Timmy did not need this treatment. Though he knew when it was better not to say anything, he was not only capable, but also tragically accustomed to facing harsh realities. When there was only one cloth-wrapped package of meat left in the freezer, enough for a day or two if we stretched it, I decided to discuss the problem with Timmy and ask him what he thought we should do. I wanted our situation to be mutually understood and any determination we made to be mutually arrived at, because his life would be as much on the line as my own. I didn't want to mince words; he deserved to know all the facts.

And so I initiated the conversation; half-buried recollections of *Lord of the Flies* danced uneasily through my mind throughout the dialogue:

"We're almost out of food, Timmy." I said somberly.

"Yeah, I know."

"I've been thinking about it for a while... I want to know what you think we should do."

"What are my choices?" he asked, rather sardonically.

I outlined our paltry options, explaining that we could quietly starve, or we could go outside and risk being feasted upon. Either way, we were likely to end up zombified.

"So, you're basically asking how I want to die," he said.

"Yes."

"Well, I'd really prefer not to..."

I nodded. There was a lump in my throat.

"If we stay here, we'll definitely die. But if we go out for food, we'll only probably die." he reasoned.

"But the way we die will probably be substantially more horrible." Though this was true, I was primarily playing devil's advocate. I didn't want to give up my last speck of hope either.

"Yes, but there's a chance we could live, at least for a while."

"I could go, and bring food back," I suggested.

"No. You don't know what it's like out there, Adrienne"

"Neither of us do."

"That's true, but what if you can't get back? Anyway, I want to stay with you... Besides," he said, "I'm an extra gun."

I smiled. Having a nine-year-old for backup didn't make me feel a whole lot more confident, but it definitely touched my heart.

Chapter 8

We prepared to leave. I was scared, but inexplicably excited at the same time—perhaps it was just the prospect of escaping the stale, acrid air of the apartment. We gathered our weapons, haphazardly attaching what we couldn't carry to belt-loops. Since Timmy's mom and dad had taken any flashlights or candles that might have previously existed in the apartment, we broke up some of the furniture, wrapping one end of each fragment with strips of clothing from Constance's closet. We put these makeshift torches and our one prized lighter (a relic retained from my smoking days, inexplicably found in my jeans pocket) in a duffel bag we found in the back of Timmy's closet. There really wasn't much else to take. We were ready.

Timmy got up on the remnants of a chair and checked the hallway through the peephole. "Looks clear," he said.

Pulling the chair back, I tentatively opened the door. The hallway was indeed clear. I led the way, shotgun in hand.

Part 2: Searching to Destroy

"I'm a street-walking cheetah
with a heart full of napalm.
I'm a runaway child
of the nuclear A-bomb.

Look out, honey,
'cause I'm using technology.
Ain't got time
to make no apology...

...I am the world's forgotten boy,
The one who's searching,
searching to destroy..."

—"Search and Destroy," Iggy and the Stooges

Chapter 9

The apartment building was a shambles. The hallways were stained and smelly, littered with debris no one would want to inspect. I saw what I was pretty sure was a bloated torso in the elevator, which miraculously worked. The lobby was worse.

Bloody handprints covered the walls and the glass entrance. Everything was overturned, and I spied a twitching corpse pinned under a security desk. We circumvented the rubble and headed for the glass door.

I grasped the handle with a finger, trying to touch it as little as possible, and opened the door. Stepping out, Timmy and I stopped abruptly. We stood and gawked.

The world outside was a disaster. It was perfectly plain that society, as we had known it, was no more. The sun was shining dispassionately down upon half-demolished residential buildings and a carpet of ambiguous trash and discarded scraps of human beings. In fact, a good portion of a human limb rested not a foot from where we stood.

Putting an arm around Timmy, I led him away.

"I don't know the city. Where should we go?" I asked him.

"There's a major street at that intersection..." he said, pointing. It was clear that neither of us had a clue what we were doing.

We pointed ourselves in the direction Timmy had indicated, and started to climb through the rubble. It was slow going. We had to choose our footing carefully to avoid protruding nails and soft tissues. The mound of debris was unstable and both of us lost our footing several times along the way.

Finally, we reached the intersection. The intersecting street was not a residential one; it was decidedly less cluttered, littered mostly with glass from jagged storefronts. Mentally giving a nod to every post-apocalyptic sci-fi film I had ever seen for their intense realism, I consoled myself with the knowledge that I would now never have to pay off my student loans as we walked past the husks of previously viable shops. All of the shops had been looted—if it counted as looting when there was no one left from whom to steal.

We rested in front of an electronics store. Eventually, Timmy decided to wander into it; I called warnings after him, begging him to be careful. When he reemerged, he was carrying a CD boom box.

Intrigued, we spent a good portion of the day hunting down batteries. We found some in a ransacked grocery; batteries were about all that was still available there. A few perishables remained, but they had perished. All the canned goods were long gone, along with pet food, and anything else that was vaguely consumable. The store still did have a wide selection of household-cleaning products though—and a couple of packs of batteries.It seemed ironic to me that all the possessions that people had struggled to own (stereos,televisions, game systems, reclining chairs and so forth) were now readily available, but the most basic commodity—food—was impossible to procure. It struck me that the human race was rather pathetic. We took the batteries and set out to the music store.

The music store was dark; all of its light fixtures had been busted out. Fortunately, enough sunlight was filtering in for us to see, so we set about picking out CD's. Timmy's tastes were appalling to me.

"Oasis?!" I exclaimed, horrified.

"Yeah, they're really cool."

"In ten years you'll be embarrassed to admit you ever liked them. It'll be like saying you liked the Romantics."

"Who?" he asked.

"Exactly!" I said. Searching for another example, I suggested,"…or *Journey.*" I emphasized the name, relishing my own cruelty.

Timmy grimaced. "But, in Oasis, the lead singer, he…"

"Shhh!" I cut him off. I had heard a noise.

At first Timmy looked hurt that I had silenced him. Then he heard it too. It sounded like something bumping into things, and it was coming from the back room. I motioned to Timmy to get back, which he did reluctantly.

As I approached the door, something on the other side began throwing itself against it. The thumping grew more furious with each step I took toward it. By the time I reached it, the body on the other side was slamming itself against the door at a superhuman pace. Merely out of habit, I reached for the doorknob, though I was sure it was locked. To my great surprise, the knob turned, and the door swung open. A rancid and highly agitated corpse fell out at me, landing squarely on the floor next to my feet. It was so excited that it was shaking. It tried to reach for me while it was still trying to pick itself up, which resulted in it doing neither adequately. It teetered on its knees, arms flapping; every time it tried to lift itself to its feet, it would lose its balance again. Its teeth chattered, clacking together in its skull. I could unfortunately see the jaw muscles at work; they were clearly visible between sparse patches of skin.

I aimed the shotgun and fired. Bits of head rained across the store as I toppled over backwards. The shotgun's kick had thrown me, bruising the hell out of my shoulder in the process. It was a real monster of a gun; firing it was more harrowing than the zombies were! I tucked it into my belt as best I could and resolved to stick with the handgun.

The zombie's behavior dumbfounded me. These creatures were apparently so stupid that they couldn't figure out that they needed to turn a goddamned doorknob.

This is what had decimated our cities? Zombies were dumber than dirt! Nor were they highly coordinated. What the hell was wrong with us?

The zombie was sporting a store apron, poor schmuck. I followed an unwise impulse to lift up its smock; below, its chest cavity lay open. Its internal organs were pure mush.

Its abhorrent physiology suggested to me that the poor sod must have been trying to eat simply out of habit, for it certainly couldn't be a productive venture; it had no intact organs with which to process flesh. Still, it had been truly hungry! It reminded me of an experiment evil bio-psychologists had commonly conducted upon dogs. They performed an "esophageal fistula" by removing an animal's esophagus. Motivation theorists the world over had chortled over the discovery that starved dogs would continue to eat, though the food dropped ineffectually into a bucket beneath their sorry necks. Therefore, I extrapolated that a hungry zombie would still want to eat, even if it couldn't process the food. Had I really needed to know this?

I shuddered, remembering that, although "proven" long before, psych grad-students had regularly performed the esophageal fistula procedure, along with other diabolical experiments, (for practice, I guess) in the "Pain Lab" at my university.

Sometimes I found it hard to lament humankind's fate.

The zombie's rotten spots, greenish hue, and general state of decomposition clearly bespoke that he was long spoiled, so we finished making our music selections and returned to the street. We took turns playing our CD's. I played a lot of atmospheric music, particularly Nine Inch Nails, figuring that Trent Reznor had created the music with a situation exactly like ours in mind. We spent the rest of the day huddled in front of a ruined storefront, listening to music and wondering if there was anything left on which for us to feed.

Chapter 10

Nighttime posed a dilemma. I was afraid that if I slept, we would become something's breakfast. I considered sleeping in shifts, but I couldn't burden Timmy with that kind of responsibility. So I stayed up the night.

Sometime during the wee hours, I heard noises—voices! Perhaps this city wasn't so dead after all. A few of the street lamps were still functioning, providing dim illumination, but it was the kind of lighting that played tricks with the eyes. I retreated further into the shadows and squinted to see.

The voices were getting louder. I considered waking Timmy, but he was sleeping soundly, his body firmly tucked into a recess in the building. I knew the niche made him practically invisible from the street, so I figured it was best for him to stay put for the moment.

Four figures emerged from the darkness; they were heading toward us. As they drew nearer, I could discern that all four were men. I couldn't decide how great a threat the group might pose to us. They looked scruffy, but then, everyone was scruffy these days. I mean, really, who felt like shaving? There was no one to keep up appearances for, and personal hygiene was not high on one's "to do" list in times of extreme crisis. Honestly, I was a bit scraggly myself.

They were carrying flashlights and one of them was hauling a large sack across his back. I thought I could make out guns on their hips. The two in front were talking.

I could only catch snippets of the conversation.

"...never find anything of use in that bin..."

"...plant..."

"...man..."

"...religion..."

"...dumpster..."

It was all gibberish to me. I must have leaned too far out of the shadows in my attempt to eavesdrop though, because one of them spotted me. I tried to submerge myself back into the gloom, but it was too late. The man gestured to his friends, and they all turned and stared. Beams of light probed the darkness, alighting on various parts of me. Then they began to approach. I was clutching my revolver so tightly that my hand began to throb.

I was heavily outnumbered and, since they were living, they did not seem to suffer from any of the handicaps that zombies fortunately tended to possess, such as slow, erratic movement or acute witlessness. Assessing the situation, I decided my best approach was to be excessively polite. I tucked the gun into the front of my jeans and took a deep breath.

"Hi. It's so good to see people!" I said, stepping out into the light of the street lamps.

"Well, that sounded dippy," I thought to myself. Nonetheless, having embarked upon this socially awkward course of action, I pressed forward.

"How's it going?" I continued, doing the best Polly Anna impression I could muster.

They crowded around me. I couldn't tell who was speaking.

"It's a girl," one of them pronounced.

I bristled slightly at being labeled such a thing, but attempted to conceal any irritation.

"You're an American, aren't you? An American! You hear that, Ray?" the youngest of the men exclaimed.

The man apparently named Ray drew forward, nodding enthusiastically and exclaiming "Ain't that something!"

He was grinning broadly, looking at me intently—almost hungrily.

Ray was a big man with a square jaw and a crew cut. He sported a couple of crude monochrome tattoos on his forearms; what they depicted, at least to me, was indiscernible. He looked like he was in his mid to late twenties and was wearing a torn and stained undershirt that had probably once been white. Both his face and chest were wide and muscular. I instantly found him creepy.

Ray was apparently from the U.S. From the pleased look on his wide, doltish face, I gathered that our shared nationality held some great significance to him. Evidently this trait linked us inextricably together.

"How old are you?" Ray inquired.

"Now there's a pressing question," I thought. I was beginning to feel like an exhibit in a zoo.

"Twenty-five."

My answer was apparently acceptable to Ray; he was beaming.

"Is that boy yours?" the youngest one asked.

The question was oddly phrased, and I wasn't sure how to answer it.

"We're together..." I said.

"You mean he's alive?" Now Ray seemed disturbed.

"Yes..." I said it slowly, drawing it out for emphasis.

"Forgive us. Of course he is." The man in front interjected. He seemed to have decided to take charge and direct the conversation down a more civil path. I was glad.

He introduced himself: "My name is John."

John's appearance sharply contrasted Ray's. He was tall, slim, and seemed to possess a calm, almost quiet, demeanor. His voice, even and melodic, had a soothing quality, and his clothes were miraculously free of grime. In fact, in light of present circumstances, his grooming in general was rather impeccable. And his eyes... his eyes were striking, and they seemed unexpectedly kind. He was actually very attractive, though I was irritated with myself for noticing.

"Adrienne." I responded.

"Have you eaten?" he asked me.

I somehow felt like this was a trick question. Perhaps my mother had read "Hansel and Gretel" to me one too many times. But then I reminded myself that I was constantly making analogies between literature and my real life. In fact, art sometimes seemed more real to me than life did. I reassured myself that I was just crazy.

"Not recently," I answered.

"Well, perhaps you and your friend would like to join us."

There was a brief rumbling of dissension among the other men, but they seemed to accept John's decision to feed us. He was obviously the leader of the group.

My stomach had been complaining for a while, and I could think of no polite way to decline anyway, so I roused Timmy.

Chapter 11

I followed the band of men, Timmy in tow.

We accompanied them, tromping through debris for a good half-hour before we reached a stopping point.

Our destination was a rickety lean-to constructed against the one intact wall of a burned out building. I couldn't fathom *why* anyone would choose such a location, yet they had.

Depositing us in what they referred to as "the courtyard," the men immediately embarked upon various tasks. Before long, one of the men, the youngest one, who looked as though he was maybe twenty or twenty-one years old, returned. He had long, brown hair, a goatee that needed to be trimmed, and wore a smug expression. He introduced himself as Congruity.

"Excuse me?" I said, confounded.

"My parents were into the whole 'flower power' thing." he said dismissively.

"Were they math majors?" I ventured, suppressing a smile.

Ignoring the question, he mumbled "Just call me Con, it's easier."

He turned to Timmy. "I could use some help. Would you like to give me a hand?" he asked.

Timmy agreed, nodding, so I was left standing alone outside the hovel, feeling purposeless.

I stood there, feeling foolish as I busied myself with picking at my fingernails. It was appalling how dirty they were.

"So, what's your story?"

The voice made me jump. I turned around. It was John.

"Oh, you startled me," I said, carrying on my new practice of saying the inane.

"The food will be ready soon," he said, smiling. I liked the way the skin around his eyes bunched up when he smiled.

"Hungry?" he asked.

"Yes." I replied, smiling back awkwardly.

"Tell me," John queried, "How have you been feeding yourselves, you and the boy?"

The question made me nervous and ashamed. Perhaps these men had been subsisting on a supply of canned goods; I certainly couldn't presume that cannibalism was the norm.

My face was hot. Hesitantly, I admitted, "We ate some bodies..."

My voice was so low that he asked me to repeat it. I wanted to sink into the ground. Talk about social stigma! I said it again.

"Everyone's a cannibal." he responded casually.

At any other time, I would have considered this a philosophical statement. Under the circumstances, I took it at face value. Depraved though it was, I was relieved to know the behavior in which I had indulged was commonplace.

"What's your relationship to the boy?" he inquired. He had drawn nearer and was now standing closer than I felt comfortable with. I began to wonder about the quality of my breath.

"I guess you could say that I'm kind of a surrogate sister to him."

"Oh. So you're not related?"

"No."

"Mmmm." he said, processing the information.

"You know, the living aren't necessarily any more trustworthy than the dead." he advised me. "Approaching anyone could be dangerous these days, especially with the boy."

"Timmy? Why do you say that?"

"There aren't many survivors, as far as I've been able to ascertain. But the ones that do exist tend to be desperate. Most of them have abandoned, um, let's say, conventional etiquette. In other words, they make no distinction between the living and the dead; a meal is a meal... And the boy is an easy mark." he added. "Is he sick?"

"No..." I said hesitantly. I appreciated his candor; he was presenting himself to me as a much-needed ally, so I calculated that it was best to continue being honest. "Well, possibly anemic, but nothing fatal," I explained.

"Hmm, well, he looks unwell—unnaturally skinny. You bring him out with you and there will be very few who won't feel justified eating him."

I gave him a perplexed look.

"People don't die of natural causes anymore. If you're sick, you're food, even among the most cultured of circles. The rationale is that if you go off and die, not only do you become a zombie—an enemy—but the living miss their window of opportunity before you spoil."

"Very pragmatic." I said weakly.

He shrugged and turned around to go back into the shack.

"Hey," I said, unwilling to let the conversation end yet.

He looked back, raising his eyebrows.

"Do you know how this started?"

"What?"

"The whole thing. The dead rising up and roaming the earth, that whole thing."

"Your guess is as good as mine." He said it with an air of resignation. With that, he turned again and departed.

And so I was left alone with my thoughts while the rest of them scampered about. Ray and the fourth man, a black man I hadn't been introduced to, were gathering plywood. Con briefly emerged from the shanty with a bottle of Worcestershire sauce.

I leaned against the lone brick column that sat in the middle of the "courtyard," a cleared area in front of the hut, and engrossed myself in thought.

No one seemed to know why the dead had decided to wander the earth. The biblical phrase "Judgment Day" came to mind, but I sensed that this was a rather perverted interpretation. It sure as hell was a fucking apocalypse though. If god had been a part of my belief system, I would probably have believed that this was a divinely devised scourge meant to punish man for his consumption of man. Was a zombie devouring a human any crueler than European settlers intentionally infecting Native Americans with smallpox? Or than Nazi Germany? Or the Khmer Rouge? Stalin? The Spanish Inquisition? The list of man's not just inhumanity to, but *consumption* of, man was endless... Sometimes I thought that studying history had destroyed the last modicum of faith I had ever placed in humanity, and that I might have been happier ignorant.

The religious theme was an obvious one for our situation, though I had never bothered to explore it before. I would have wagered that the evangelical types had had a real field day with the "Judgment Day" motif. I bet that they were feeling oh-so righteous right about now, if any of them still survived. I'd never understood why man had constructed religion to provide order, and then used it to divide himself. I was sure that hate-mongers must have practically salivated when presented with the opportunity to use this blight to further the agendas of their own narrow, intolerant ideologies. I could just hear them blaming the existence of zombies upon the existence of homosexuals, interracial couples, or unwed mothers. Metaphorically, those sanctimonious bastards had been sustaining themselves on the flesh of "sinners" all along. Bitterly, I hoped that none of them *had* survived.

Chapter 12

The men had accumulated a decent-sized pile of boards in the courtyard. John returned and lit a fire.

Con came and placed several large chunks of marinated meat on a slipshod spit. It smelled exquisite, and soon all of us were congregated around the bonfire.

Timmy came and sat by me. He looked tired. I put an arm around him and rested my chin on his head. The meat-fat was crackling as the flames licked the roasting food. Ray was humming monotonously. John was sitting directly across from me with Con at his right shoulder. They were talking about A-levels and O-levels. I tuned the conversation out; the English educational system was something I'd given up on trying to understand long before. The black man was sitting apart from the rest of the group. He reclined silently, staring into the fire. He was an attractive man, maybe thirty years old, with bright, smooth skin and shoulder-length braided hair. He looked distant. It occurred to me that I hadn't heard him speak all night.

It was somehow peaceful to watch the fire, surrounded by living people.

When the meat was cooked, Con removed it from the fire and doled it out to us. The food was good, and I ate enthusiastically. The men ate with even more gusto; when they were finished with the flesh, they cracked open the bones and sucked the marrow.

"Goldfish mentality," John explained, detecting my mild dismay. "You have to consume as much as you possibly can when you don't know when the next meal is coming." He smiled.

Timmy and I followed their lead, breaking open the bones, downing every last morsel.

Almost as soon as we finished our meal, Timmy lay down behind me and went back to sleep. It amazed me how quickly that child could pass into slumber. I envied it.

Everyone remained around the fire, savoring the heat of the pyre.

Con addressed me. "Adrienne, you seem strangely on-edge."

"I've been on-edge since I saw my first zombie." I replied.

This didn't seem to satisfy him. He looked skeptical, and I didn't want him to spread misgivings about me to the rest of the group.

I tried to dispel any reason for suspicion, replying casually, "I mean, who would have thought zombies really existed? It's a bit of a mind-fuck."

"Well, actually," Con said, "zombies occur in folktales of all cultures. Didn't you think there was a reason for that?"

"No, I always figured that vampires, werewolves, and zombies were all universal symbols, part of a Jungian collective subconscious..." my voice trailed off.

We all sat for a moment in silence, gazing into the fire.

"I guess I was wrong." I concluded.

John entered the discussion. "Maybe they *are* just a metaphor of the subconscious. Maybe we are all just dreaming," he suggested wistfully.

"Maybe it's just me that is asleep, and you're all just part of my demented dream...". I said, though I didn't mean to say it. I thought it, and it unintentionally slipped out.

"Christ!" John exclaimed. "For all of our sakes, I wish you'd wake up!"

We all chuckled, nodding our heads in agreement.

"So you're an American," Ray said.

"Oh, god, not this again." I thought to myself. Hadn't we covered this? I almost had to feel sorry for Ray. Rehashing this topic was the only way he could find to break into the conversation.

"Yes." I said.

He grinned sheepishly.

"What part?"

"South." I said. I didn't feel like getting too specific.

"Huh, me too!" he said gleefully.

"Oh, really?" I said, feigning surprise.

The conversation languished.

"How did you get here?" he resumed.

Perhaps I was being unfair, but I couldn't shake the sense that Ray was dangerous—that violence lingered just below his surface, ready to bubble up at any moment. He seemed utterly transparent, dim-witted, and horny. I was rapidly growing to resent his assumption that being from the same country meant I wanted to associate with him. Sharing in common a country of origin (especially when it was a large country) was not a legitimate excuse for making conversation.

"I don't know." I answered less than congenially.

John began to eye me with suspicion.

"How could you not know?" asked Ray.

"My guess is that I had some kind of trauma-induced fugue, or maybe a psychotic break... I just woke up here."

I couldn't resist privately smirking to myself; my answer was totally unintelligible to Ray.

"So you're saying you're 'Tabula Rosa'" Con said. He seemed to have something to prove. He added, condescendingly, "That means a blank slate. According to John Locke, we're all blank slates at birth."

Perhaps Con found women threatening when they weren't fluff-chicks. Perhaps he thought all Americans were uneducated. Or perhaps he just had to prove that he knew more than anyone else. At that time, I couldn't resist the bait. .

"I'm familiar with the theory," I said coldly. Even if I weren't, would that have made me an invalid human being?

"But no," I continued, "I still have a fully developed sense of self, I don't need to relearn things or figure out who I am. I remember everything from before, just nothing about the

91

zombies. Life was normal, then I woke up here in England, and there were zombies."

"Well, that sounds likely."Con snorted. "Maybe you and Briton should have a talk," he said, gesturing toward the quiet man.

Ray laughed.

"Briton hasn't talked since it started," explained John. "He was a successful businessman, a spokesperson; he talked for a living."

Ray snickered loudly; his behavior implied that he found Briton's success inconceivable.

John ignored him, continuing, "...But apparently the trauma was too much." He dropped his voice. "His whole family was eaten."

He ceased speaking for a moment. I thought he was finished, but then he motioned for me to come across to him; he didn't want to repeat whatever he had to say within earshot of Briton.

I skirted the blaze and sat down next to him.

He proceeded to whisper the rest of the story to me.

"When I found him," he began, "the house was a bloodbath. It was just horrible... bloody horrible." He looked pained; he clenched his jaw and squeezed his eyes shut for a moment. His facial expressions clearly conveyed to me just how horrendous the scene must have been.

I nodded, acknowledging that I understood.

He regained his composure quickly. "His wife, his mother, even his infant son... they'd all been eaten to death. His wife had lost an entire arm! Well, you know what happens when people die. He had to bash in their skulls—and who could blame him? When I found him, he was standing over the bassinet, just rocking back and forth." He paused. "I don't think crushing the baby's skull sat well with him."

I cringed.

"Hasn't said a word since," he concluded.

I sat there for a while, chewing on my lower lip. Then I returned to my spot alongside Timmy. Absentmindedly, I brushed his fine hair from his forehead and sat looking at him for a while.

The group talked a bit longer around the fire. More accurately, Con spoke fervently, pointedly addressing only John, and I managed to slip a couple of questions in to them.

Their answers did furnish me with a few details I hadn't previously known about the zombie situation. Apparently, the living in the U.S. had gone underground (it struck me as mildly ironic to go underground to escape the dead). In Northern Ireland, the living's tastes were discriminating; surviving Catholics were eating surviving Protestants and vice versa. In Great Britain, the zombies were pretty much gone. They had pillaged everything and, when nothing remained, they left in search of greener pastures. The rest of Europe had been holding its own, but the undead plague spread through it like wildfire once the zombies found the tunnels.

The few zombies that remained in England were apparently just too stupid to figure out how to leave.

I tried to ask if anyone knew what had happened in cultures that cremated their dead, but Con cut me off every time I began. Finally, I got the question in:

"What about the East? Have the zombies won there too? Buddhists cremate their dead, don't they?" I spat into Con's soliloquy about the rare opportunity the potential demise of social norms offered us.

John, who seemed thankful for the momentary diversion, answered, "Reanimation started in the West and spread. Who knows? Maybe it will fizzle out when the hordes get to Asia. People might be able to fend them off there. Hopefully, they can eliminate the Western swarm. They do cremate their own dead."

"I guess it really will be the Pacific Century," I mused to myself.

Con went back to vocalizing his own speculations. As the evening wound down, the men began to recount their favorite zombie anecdotes:

"…it sounded like it was yodeling! Who knows if they're capable of thought." Con was saying. "All we really know is that their speech centers shut down almost immediately. They could be fucking Einsteins, but they sure as hell can't communicate it."

"Their peripheral vision is the first thing to go." John stated. "I once walked behind one for a good twenty minutes. It attacked every poor chap that got in front of it, but it was totally oblivious to my presence."

I considered trying to share my doorknob story, but I was too tired. I leaned back and let their voices run together, drifting off into much needed sleep.

Chapter 13

That night, I dreamed that I visited my therapist. Keeping my eyes firmly fixed upon the floor, I confided to her that I had been consuming human flesh. Then I noticed smacking noises. I looked up and saw that she was eating. She daintily wiped the corners of her mouth with a napkin. I glanced at the desk behind her; a cafeteria tray rested upon it. The tray held a plastic bowl, and the bowl contained a half-eaten hand.

"Extreme circumstances justify extreme actions, Adrienne" she said, taking a bite from a finger as though it were a chicken wing. "When in Rome…"

Chapter 14

When I woke up, the sun was high in the sky, and the fire was out. Everyone was still asleep, save the living embodiment of anti-intellectualism himself, Ray. He followed me around all afternoon; our conversations were banal at best and instantly forgettable. It took every ounce of tact I could rally to conceal the disdain I felt for him. Eventually, the rest of the group arose.

Mercifully, Ray joined the other men, though he soon returned to inform me that they would be going out "huntin'", and that Timmy and I should remain in the encampment. I met the hunter-gatherer aspect of this proposal with indignation, but I accepted it. It would only ruffle feathers if I went along. Besides, Timmy couldn't afford to be seen, and I didn't want to leave him alone in the camp. So, I resigned myself to let their archaic schema remain intact. Timmy and I would benefit from their labor, so I let it be.

Before they left, John came to check in on me.

He sat down next to me, cross-legged, and asked, "All set? You have ample ammo, just in case?"

I confirmed that I was fine.

He seemed lost in thought for a moment. Then he abruptly said, "Alright then," and was on his feet again.

Searching for something meaningless and polite to close with, I said, "See you later."

Standing behind me, he reached down and clasped my shoulder, squeezing it tightly for a moment, then releasing.

Puzzled, I turned around, but he was gone.

I was surprised by this small, but sudden, expression of affection from John.

After they left, I was alone with my thoughts and spent some time pondering John.

He was perhaps forty and rather handsome, in a roguish sort of way. He was nearly six-foot and slim, and his skin had a rather pleasant, leathery quality. His face housed cold blue eyes and was framed by sandy brown hair that had undoubtedly once been confined in a business-cropped style, but had long since grown out, escaping to his shoulders.

A well-spoken man, he was, at least on the surface, only slightly roughened by his experiences. He had a wry way of putting things that I found appealing, though I wasn't sure if I should just attribute this trait to him being English. Honestly, he was rather charming, perhaps even a tad dashing.

He had divulged very little about his previous life. I thought I had heard someone mention that he had been divorced. I wasn't sure. No one spoke much about the past here and, truthfully, there was no point in dredging it up. We were defined only by what we were today. Who we had been before was no longer important, only painful to remember.

Still, John's background weighed on my mind. When we had first met, I had wanted to imagine

John as a working-class hero. His speech and mannerisms soon betrayed his aristocratic heritage, however. I had always adapted well to other cultures or customs, but class divisions still threw me into culture shock. Having been born into urban poverty, I was not versed in the etiquette required to blend in with even the upper-middle class, and I resented the concept of entitlement as birthright too much to ever make any attempt to learn. So John was really too posh for my tastes—too polished, though current circumstances had certainly begun to fray him around the edges. Still, he had most certainly had it all—a good upbringing, prestigious schools (Oxford, I think I had heard him say over the campfire), and I'm sure a string of whatever the English equivalent of debutantes was. I made myself dismiss it. He was the closest thing to an adult ally I had, and now wasn't the time to resent money. For once, money made no difference. Still, it bothered me that it had taken the collapse of society to equalize us all. Had the lumpen masses really been so complacent that this was the closest

Western society would come to parity? It probably was. If the living prevailed, I thought, we would quickly resurrect a new hierarchy, and John would probably go back to dining with snooty aunts and pretentious uncles, while the rest of us struggled to purchase small diversions to distract us from our circumstances.

"What are you thinking about?" Timmy broke in on my thoughts.

I roused myself back to reality, such as it was.

"Nothing." I said.

Chapter 15

The men returned empty-handed, so we ate what was left of the previous night's meal, "Fred." The leftovers were decidedly less enticing—innards and digits and genitals; our mood was more solemn than the night before. None the less, Con persisted in carrying on a lively conversation—it was a rant, really, in which he denounced just about everything that came to his mind..

"—it's a prime example of capitalism eating itself!" he shouted.

I was beginning to learn everyone's foibles. An ardent Marxist, Con was staunchly self-involved, an over-zealous college student, and a condescending bastard. His favorite past-times were cooking and arguing—he loved to start "debates" as an excuse to yell at people and flaunt his self-perceived genius.

"Our society," he raved, "had no redeeming qualities—none whatsoever! We produced nothing of value. But now, now we have now stripped ourselves free of pretense. I, for one, embrace this autonomy—this new freedom from decadence!"

For some reason, though I should have known better, he sucked me in.

"I'm from Generation X," I said. "I'm *supposed* to be cynical and nihilistic..." I paused. "And I am," I qualified. "But I can't condemn *all* of pre-zombie society. I mean, what about art? Music? Literature?"

"What about it?" he said contemptuously.

"Well, for instance, there were some really excellent independent film-makers—hell, even the Simpsons was a damned good show." I was circling my point, unable to close in.

He leaped on that. "You're saying that modern civilization was worthwhile because of the *entertainment*?" His outrage was quite convincing.

"It was nothing more than the *opiate of the masses*!" he spat.

"How often have you even seen poverty portrayed in the movies?"

"That was about willing suspension of disbelief—the majority of audiences weren't *willing*; they didn't *want* to see poor people. It didn't sell because they weren't buying."

"Are you calling the masses mindless chattel?" he shouted condemningly.

In a sense, I probably was. People generally don't want to be reminded of reality. I wouldn't have wanted to watch a zombie movie right about now myself.

I said nothing for a moment.

Inhaling deeply, I began again. "Forget mass-marketed entertainment. I'm talking about art. Haven't you ever seen a movie or heard a song that defined you—that encapsulated your beliefs?"

"The *Simpsons* defined you?" he asked, mockingly agape.

He was eyeing me ostentatiously. Damn, he was pig-headed. He was just too damned cool. Nobody had ever been as clued-in as he was; nobody but him was apparently even capable of expressing valid thoughts. Arrogant bastard.

In the midst of a zombie apocalypse, I really shouldn't have cared about one egomaniacal college kid, but I suppose I needed somewhere to channel my anger. Call it transference.

"No. I think you're missing the point," I sighed. "Nothing ever touched you, or perhaps made you laugh with it at the absurdity of life?"

"Life is a serious matter." he said caustically.

My god, how dismally dull. "Con" should have been short for Contrary.

I gave it a final stab. "Art can capture something we know is true, but are unable to articulate. Movies, books, paintings... art in general—it can act as commentary on the world around us and add to our own experience. It adds to who we are. I don't think that's necessarily pacification."

"It's all false consciousness!" he spluttered.

I shrugged; his interpretation of Marx was only meant to fit the argument of the moment.

"Maybe it is... " I said abjectly. "But it was at least a quality drug. Maybe it was all about the experience—it made us happy. It was part of us."

"Libertine!" he scoffed, sneering victoriously.

This was the last time I tried to converse with Con. If he thought the world was better now, he was welcome to it.

After the meal, we all retired. Without saying a word, John leaned back and laid his head in my lap. That was the extent of it; he closed his eyes and fell asleep resting on me. I was stunned. I felt as though I should be offended by his audacity, but I couldn't muster it. Despite all the pent-up rage I wanted to focus upon him, I found him a compelling enigma. I stroked his hair as he slumbered, my hand trembling ever so slightly as I drew out each strand, as if I might be overwhelmed at any moment and fall into convulsions if I belied even the hint of emotion. I steadied my hand and continued to caress his hair, in measured, controlled strokes.

I am not sure when I finally slipped off into sleep that night, but when I did, I dreamed we were all sitting around the fire eating a hardy meal of tacks. Con and Ray and Timmy and I were all downing them quite adeptly, but Briton's mouth began to stream with blood as he chewed.

Always detached, John declined the meal.

Chapter 16

The next day's hunt was as fruitless as the previous one, and we had no leavings left to pick over. The day after was the same. The mood in the camp grew progressively more grim.

John continued to confound me, randomly massaging my shoulders or twisting a lock of my hair between his fingers, but rarely saying anything at all. I *was* attracted to him. Though I found his aloofness annoying, is his allure was still undeniable.

I briefly considered the possibility of a romance between us, but soon surmised that it would be too much trouble. In a different life, where zombies were merely fiction, I would have fallen for him—though without the undead scourge, I would never have any reason to meet him in the first place. But here, in reality, I was too tired, if not too proud, to pursue someone so remote. Hell, I was probably too remote for a relationship myself. I had always imagined that people felt compelled to cling to one another in stressful times, but, on the contrary, I felt estranged; my desire was to withdraw from others. I didn't have the emotional energy to expend on the ups and downs of a new romance, nor did I have any desire to add additional names to the roster of people I cared about.

He and I continued to not discuss any of this, and we quietly starved, just like everybody else.

Part 3: Ray is an American

"Johnny's in America,
no one needs anyone,
they don't even just pretend...

I'm afraid of Americans,
I'm afraid of the world,
I'm afraid I can't help it...

...God is an American."

—"I'm Afraid of Americans," David Bowie

Chapter 17

On the fifth day, only three of them returned.

"Where's Briton?" I asked of Ray.

"Zombie got him. Came up on him suddenly. Wasn't anything we could do."

The news saddened me. Briton had been the easiest one to get along with in the bunch.

"On the bright side, dinner's on." Ray said. He was all smiles.

I generally found Ray repulsive, but his cheery demeanor really chilled me.

I got up and stepped into the hut. Sure enough, Briton's body was resting on the scaffold Con used to prepare the meals, his limbs still fettered together to facilitate easy hauling. There was something wrong with the picture though. Except for the bullet wound in his temple, Briton looked remarkably unsullied. Where were the gaping wounds? A zombie would have had to maul him pretty badly to kill him, wouldn't it?

I stepped back outside. I didn't tell Timmy my suspicion, though he immediately sensed that something was upsetting me and repeatedly asked.

Shortly after dinner, I caught John and asked him what had happened to Briton.

He just shook his head. I persisted until he divulged, "I wasn't there. We had split up. You'd have to ask Ray."

At mealtime, I reluctantly took a seat. I felt guilty as hell, but I was hungry.

Ray served the meal that night. He gave me my portion with a smile, quipping "I hope you like dark meat!"

I recoiled. Was there a more foul being on the planet than Ray? That racist fiend had killed him, and now he was making jokes about it!

He set the plate down next to me and moved on.

I want to say that I didn't partake in Briton. I really wish that I could, but I can't. I was convinced Ray had murdered him, and I was vehemently revolted. But Briton was already dead. Utilitarianism got the best of me.

Chapter 18

After everyone was asleep, I extricated myself from John (he had made a pillow of my leg) and woke Timmy.

"What? What is it, Adrienne?"

"We're leaving, Timmy. We're leaving right now." I was so anxious I was hissing the words.

"But why?" he asked, rubbing the sleep from his eyes.

"I'll tell you after we leave. We need to go *now*."

Timmy knew I wasn't prone to issuing random commands, so he took my words seriously. He got up quickly, grabbing the blanket he had been using, and trailed after me.

I popped into the lean-to and stole a flashlight.

"Should we take some food?" he whispered.

"No." I said. It was easier to be ethical on a full stomach.

Then we were off.

Chapter 19

We wandered for days, maybe weeks; there was no food to be found. Most of the city was out of power now, so we lived in almost constant darkness. To complete the effect, it seemed to rain every day.

Timmy began to lose his color again, and the circles under his eyes grew so dark that he looked as though he had two black eyes. I became dizzy all of the time.

The situation had never been so dire.

I thought about letting Timmy eat me, a warped act of altruism, but I knew he'd just starve again once I was finished. I had to protect him, to save us.

As time passed, Timmy slept longer and longer—often close to twenty hours a day. I was so dazed half of the time that I didn't even know what I was doing; we barely escaped becoming zombie brunch on several occasions.

Then, one morning, I noticed something quite spectacular. In front of a quaint, little English bungalow stood a tree. A *fig* tree, laden with its fruit! Did fig trees even grow in the U.K.? Maybe it was a mirage; we gorged ourselves, none the less. The fruit was ripe and sweet. It was strange to eat fruit; it felt like I hadn't tasted it in a decade. And how wonderfully biblical! Awash in bizarre symbolism, reveling in this improbable moment, I gorged myself. It probably wasn't the most nutritionally complete of meals, but it filled our bellies, and it was wonderful. We both felt revived.

Undoubtedly, people had previously picked that tree clean. However, people were less plentiful these days, and glorious Mother Nature had replenished herself; I felt as though I had witnessed a mystical wonder. I kissed that damned tree.

The food enabled me to think clearly again. After taking a lazy nap, sheltered under the canopy of fig leaves, I turned resolutely to Timmy. His cheeks were already regaining their pinkish tinge.

"We have to go to the countryside." I said.

"Yes. There'll be food there." he concurred.

Chapter 20

Timmy, my little human compass, had had an aunt who lived in the countryside, so he led the way. Together, we passed from the bleak wasteland of the city, into green, fertile lands. As we entered this new world, I was struck by the simple, uncorrupted splendor of nature around us. A city person by birthright, the words "rustic charm" had always struck me as a misnomer, but now I understood.

We stayed in these pastoral surroundings for months, free of the politics of men and zombies. Timmy and I started off subsisting primarily upon berries. Tree bark and termites added variety, becoming part our diet after I remembered a news story about some soldier that had been trapped behind enemy lines and survived on such things. It wasn't haute cuisine, but neither was human flesh.

Sometimes we took refuge in one of the few cottages that dotted the terrain, though the respite was seldom as amiable as the homes' quaint exteriors suggested. Inside, they were uniformly squalid; telltale signs of the undead plight (i.e., bloodstains and fragmentary remains) were plentiful. Mostly, we used these dwellings as pit-stops for replenishing supplies; our clothes wore thin quickly, requiring constant mending and frequent replacement.

When the weather was good, we preferred to sleep in the open air. We felt safe; our rural world, as far as we could ever tell, was blissfully uninhabited. It and, by default, we, existed independently from the war between the living and the dead.

As the winter approached, food became more difficult to obtain. When the seasonal change exhausted the last of nature's bounty, we returned to the city to scavenge. I cursed my lack of foresight.

Chapter 21

The city was just as we had left it, only more lifeless. Our first few days were unproductive and mundane. I found myself half-wishing a zombie would pop up, just to create some motion, to disturb the horrid stillness of this blighted city.

A few days after we arrived in the city, we wandered into the ruins of shopping center. Timmy and I were vainly hoping for supplies or, though we didn't dare admit it aloud, nonperishable food.

Though the mall was dark, we traversed it quickly; we were anxious to get to the south end, where there was a promising shop, brimming with "sweets and pickled things," according to Timmy.

I think Timmy and I both were under the impression that the city had died during our absence. I didn't expect any difficulties.

Honestly, I wasn't paying any attention. I didn't hear anything, nor did I detect any motion in the darkness. Timmy began tugging at my sleeve.

"What?" I asked, as I walked straight into a towering, blubbery form.

I leaped back, yanking Timmy's arm back as I did so. Timmy let out a wail. I guess I had jerked too hard.

I stood frozen, squinting like hell, trying to penetrate the darkness with my eyes. I needed to see a head before I could aim for it.

"Shit. Get the lighter!" I urged Timmy.

"Hello? You're alive, I take it?" a man's voice called out. He was behind me now. I spun around.

"Don't be alarmed, dear." the voice said. Then it shouted, apparently to someone in the distance, "Stanley, would you light the fountain?"

At first, it seemed that he had uttered a non sequitur; then, suddenly, a large fire burst up from

123

what had once been an extensive mall fountain. It illuminated a vast expanse of the mall. A man of medium build stood near the warm glow of the fountain.

These two men had apparently built a bonfire out of refuse here in the mall, containing it within the remnants of the fountain.

The man that had spoken to us was portly and in his early fifties. "Frank." he said, extending his hand.

Shaking his hand, I introduced myself and Timmy.

Following Frank at his instruction, we joined the other man, Stanley, at the fire.

"Evening." said Stanley, tipping his hat.

We exchanged pleasantries for a while. Frank did most of the talking. Timmy and I were attentive, periodically nodding politely.

Frank told us that we should remain with them, at least until morning, explaining: "We pretty much occupy one end of the mall or another, but when we travel back and forth, I often find things have moved. Sometimes even blood trails. I'm not sure who, or what, else is here, but you probably would be better off with some sunlight filtering in to see by."

We heeded his advice and all turned in together.

It disturbed me that we had blindly stumbled into their camp. My senses were no longer refined; I was slipping. And, although Frank seemed affable enough, I couldn't judge the severity of the situation. Trust was tantamount to death in this world.

I slept fitfully, intermittently waking up and probing the darkness with my eyes.

Late that night, I heard Frank and Stanley talking, or maybe I dreamed it. The fire in the fountain illuminated their faces, casting ghoulish shadows and creating caverns out of their mouths as they spoke.

Stanley had taken off his hat, which now sat perched upon his knee. The light produced a halo around his wild, white hair as he bobbed his head, saying:

"… some of them were infected with something in the 1980s. It might have been in the school lunches… or maybe it was on the currency. It could have been the ink they used for the tabloid magazines."

Frank only muttered.

"It might have been a time-release bacteria." Stanley continued. He looked quite mad.

"Where did it all start? The states, right? The states and here, in the U.K., is where it all started. It had to have something to do with Thatcher. Thatcher and Reagan, I always told you…"

"We've been through this, Stan. It doesn't make any difference…" Frank responded.

"It lay dormant—then KA-POW!" Stanley exclaimed. "Now they're eating everyone else. I think you only turn into one if you've been exposed though. You'll turn. Our new guest will turn. Hell, I might too. But do you think the Queen Mother will? NO! No!" He laughed. "She always wore gloves. The Queen will never be a zombie!"

"Bullshit." Frank said. "The Queen is a zombie, just like everybody else!"

"Everyone's crazy." I consoled myself, and sank back into sleep.

Chapter 22

When I got up that morning, Stanley was not there. "Went out for cooking supplies."

Frank explained. "Where's the food?" I asked. Frank smiled and looked toward Timmy, who was still sleeping peacefully beside the fountain. "You brought it." he said. A chill ran up my spine.

I tried to talk my way out of it. "No, I think you've misinterpreted the situation," I said. "He's my charge. He's my brother," I simplified, "...my responsibility. Not a meal."

He obviously found my ploy lame. He sighed and began speaking to me as though I were hopelessly puerile.

"Look, dear, it's triage. We eat the weak to preserve the strong." he explained slowly. "It's a sound philosophy,"

It was a formative rationalization. "That puts Social Darwinism in a whole new light." I thought to myself, but held my tongue. Instead, I took a more diplomatic approach.

"But he's only weak because he is young. He could grow up to be strong, if he's given half a chance. Besides, I can get you other food..."

He was growing impatient. "No, no, dear. He's food. You're just going to have to accept it."

I buried my face in my hands. This ruse was much more effective; he turned to leave me to my tears.

Christ, he had underestimated me. He hadn't even thought to disarm me in my sleep. As he strode away, through mock tears, I said, "Frank?"

"Yes?" he asked, his back to me; he was approaching Timmy.

"I eat the strong to preserve the weak." Walking up behind him, I placed the barrel of my revolver against the back of his head.

"That's rather hypocritical, don't you think?" he said.

"We're all hypocrites," I said.

Then I pulled the trigger.

I withdrew the hunting blade from my boot. Slipping it behind the shoulder blade, I hacked off a hefty slab of him. Replacing the knife, I scooped Timmy, still bleary-eyed, up under one arm and, carrying Frank's freshly dismembered extremity in the other, I ran.

Chapter 23

We stretched out the food for as long as we could. The weather aided us; a cold snap descended suddenly, so we found accommodations indoors and left the human mutton out to freeze. We only returned to eat from it when we were very hungry every few days.

One morning Timmy awoke me early, just as the sun was surfacing in the sky. I shivered in the crisp morning air, but stirred myself speedily.

"What? What is it, Timmy?" I was disoriented. "Is something wrong?" I grew more alarmed as I acclimated to consciousness.

"No. Everything is fine, Adrienne. You worry too much. It's just something I want you to see."

I managed to stagger to my feet. Timmy impatiently grasped my hand and briskly led me out and down the block.

"You wandered off all this way while I was asleep? Timmy, that's very dangerous..." I lectured.

"Look!" Timmy interrupted, pointing.

A stooped-over figure was standing some yards away. I instinctively lurched back, pulling Timmy along with me. It was dead—full of unplumbed wounds and free of much of its epidermis. Timmy shook himself loose from me and marched forward.

"Timmy, what are you doing?" I shouted. Even as I chided him, I realized that the zombie wasn't responding. It was the damnedest thing. It stood there like a statue.

I caught up with Timmy, again pulling him away; then I approached it, guardedly.

It was just what it looked like—a zombie statue.

"He's frozen!" Timmy exclaimed happily.

He *was* frozen. He wasn't completely solid, but he was abundantly icy.

Cautiously scraping a nail across his forearm, frost flaked from him as if he were a tub of ice cream in an over-active freezer.

Feeling more daring, I looked it in the face. Examining his cold, steely eyes, I could have sworn—somehow, I knew—it was still alive, or undead, or whatever it was, in there. It was patiently waiting to thaw so it could go about its business.

"Well, hello, Frosty." I said.

"How's it going, Frosty, old boy?" Timmy chimed.

Together, we made great sport of teasing the thing; we chastised it mercilessly. We danced around the bugger and sang songs, altering lyrics, such as the seasonal standby: "Frosty, the snowman, was a very nappy soul, with a two puffy eyes and a rotting nose..." We tried "Ring Around the Zombie," but neither of us could come up with a good rhyme. Before we were finished, I launched into the old Joe Cocker favorite, "You Can Leave Your Head On," crooning "baby, take off your skin...real slow."

Timmy played along, but had no idea what I was parodying. I hoped the zombie got it.

After we had both worked ourselves into a tizzy, we collapsed in a fit of giggles at the zombie's feet. It was cheap empowerment, but I didn't care. We were impossibly juvenile; it was fantastic.

Before we abandoned the zombicicle, I thought to incapacitate it.

Timmy broke off its arms, whacking them loose with a tree branch and then tugging resolutely to yank them free, breaking through the putrid, stringy tendons that continued to hang on, still loosely connecting the appendages. Then I kicked out its legs. We figured that would slow it down.

Chapter 24

Except for cruelly taunting a hapless zombie, our days that winter were colorless, and often funereal. When we finished our allotment of Frank, we resorted to carrion we found amid the rubble. A lot of what we ate had gone to seed, and we both developed terrible diarrhea. Whenever the cramps struck, we had to hurriedly dig holes in the debris to dispose of our copious waste. The stomach spasms were so strong, sometimes we remained for hours, hunched and grimacing, our anuses still retching after they could expel no more.

Timmy and I scraped by, eating scraps we might or might not be able to hold down. Our lax bowels left us dehydrated, our skin inelastic and loose; we were pretty wretched, but we somehow survived.

The intolerable cold began to wane. As the temperature outside began to climb, our optimism lifted with it—especially Timmy's. He began to talk daily about how soon we would be able to leave the city and resume our alternate lives. I would have never imagined a child could be so happy about the prospect of eating tree bark. It made me glad to see him brightening up. He was looking healthier just from the anticipation.

How we longed for winter's end, so that we could return to our life in the countryside. If I believed in fate, I would say that it wasn't meant to be. But I don't believe in fate; I believe in dumb luck and random senselessness. Dumb luck and random senselessness were what stymied us that winter.

Chapter 25

Only about a week before the world broke into bloom, I had a dream. I have no idea what the dream meant, if anything, but the mind has a funny way of remembering stupid details surrounding major life events.

The dream was this:

I was at a swanky dinner party (a function I had never actually experienced in my real life, but such is the way dreams are).

Many important people and dignitaries were in attendance. The catch was, they were all dead. This esteemed event counted among its guests innumerous famous people, all in various states of decay. Lucille Ball was flirting with Calvin Coolidge. Desi was brooding in a corner, somehow consoled, despite the language barrier, by Napoleon Bonaparte. I kept hearing people whispering that Benito had arrived, but no one could find him. Chester Allen Arthur was milling about aimlessly. He approached me and asked if I knew why everyone was shunning him and where he could find a decent cup of tea. I disencumbered myself of Chester, dumping him on Neville Chamberlain, and found a good vantage-point in an empty corner. I surveyed the room. Marilyn Monroe, now jawless, was conversing with Einstein beside the murky punch bowl. Gandhi passed me, saying "excuse me," and proceeded to sit down cross-legged on the floor and munch on a disembodied head, spilling brains untidily around him. Stalin began shouting something about the carpet. Then Sigmund Freud crawled up to me and bit me on the leg.

Chapter 26

When I opened my eyes, John was standing over me. I closed my eyes and tried again. He was still there when I reopened them. Was I still at the dinner party of the damned? No, my surroundings were nowhere near so grandiose. I was back on terra firma alright, entrenched again in inauspicious reality...

"John?" I asked.

"Yes, hello." He spoke tenderly, but his expression was a troubled one.

"What are you doing here?" I looked around. "Where's Timmy?"

"They took him, Adrienne. I'm sorry. There was nothing I could do."

"This is a dream." I said, trying to keep myself calm.

"I'm sorry. I wish it were." he said quietly.

I dug my fingernails into my arm. I felt it. Did that really mean I was awake?

As if in a trance, I got up and gathered my things.

"Which way is your camp?" I asked him.

"Adrienne, it's too late." He grasped me by my shoulders.

"You could have stopped him... why didn't you stop him?" I was pounding my hands ineffectually against his chest, flailing weakly, mindlessly.

"He wouldn't have listened to me. I don't have any control anymore." He was speaking soothingly, but I wasn't having any of it.

"Bullshit!" I shouted, forcefully pushing him away. "He hasn't eaten Con! ...has he?" I wasn't too sure on this point, now that I had said it.

"No, he hasn't, but that's only because Ray can't cook."

"What about you? You look pretty intact!" I said.

"He doesn't really know how to think either. That makes me relatively useful; my presence makes his life easier. I'm more expendable than Con though. The immediacy of eating takes precedence over thinking in his hierarchy of needs."

"This isn't happening." I said, and I began to walk.

"Where are you going, Adrienne?" he cried after me.

"To save Timmy."

"It's too late." he gasped, catching up to me. "He'll be dead by now."

I kept going.

Following beside me, he reached out for my shoulder.

"Look, let's just make a clean break—together."

"I can't... Timmy..." Tears were stinging my eyes.

"I told you..." he said, not wanting to have to repeat it.

"I have to see for myself. We can't waste any time," I added, quickening my pace. "He may still be alive."

"And what are you going to do, Adrienne?" he asked, apparently appealing to some rationality I didn't have. "You're going to bust into camp and demand that they let him go? You'll wind up on the menu beside him!" he was speaking animatedly, passionately.

"... Or worse." he added ominously.

"I'm taking him by force." I said resolutely. "Are you going to help or not?"

"It's a suicide mission." he said.

"You don't understand. Timmy is my life—my impetus for everything. It's worth that risk to me." John couldn't seem to understand that my love for Timmy was the only thing left that still made me human.

"Look," he admitted, "I've gotten by this long without getting blood on my hands " I don't want to spill any now."

Incensed, I stopped in my tracks and spun around.

"Do you really think you can survive in this world without soiling your hands?" I was shouting; it was as though my voice were a separate entity from the rest of me. I listened to myself scream.

"Look at me!" I shouted. "I'm awash with blood!"

Regaining some control, I dropped my voice. "I'm sorry you don't have the stomach for all of this," I said stonily. "God bless your integrity." My voice dripped with sarcasm.

"Why am I wasting time talking?" I muttered, and began to walk again.

John trotted after me. He caught me and spun me around. His voice cracking, he said, "I'm sorry. I can't."

"Not shedding blood isn't an option, John." I was preaching now. My voice, gravelly with anger, had dropped so low it was barely audible.

"In this world, integrity isn't about not shedding blood—it's about whose blood you spill. I've done a lot of things I'm not proud of..." My words elicited Briton's image, but I promptly pushed it under, tucking it deeply away in my psyche.

"...but killing a couple of bastards to save Timmy," I intoned, "is the right thing to do! I couldn't live with myself if I didn't do it."

He slowly nodded his head but said nothing. Finally, he spoke. His voice was faint and thoughtful. "That's what works for you." he said. "We all have different breaking points. It's something I can't reconcile myself with."

I lashed out. "Those are some constipated values you've got there!" I pronounced. "Cognitive dissonance is one thing, but I think you'll reconcile yourself with it just fine once you're a zombie."

He remained at my side, despite my denouncements; though he would not aid me, he was intent upon escorting me to my destination.

We walked for several minutes in silence.

"You're a modern-day imperialist, Adrienne," he said finally, a smile softly tugging at the corners of his mouth, "policing the world."

"Pacifist." I responded gently. I didn't want to control the world, only to survive it. But maybe he was right. Maybe the only way I could survive in this world was to control it.

We both fell mute again and continued to walk.

"What did you mean, 'or worse'?" I asked, trying to divert attention to another subject.

He inhaled deeply, and began, "Well, you know that Ray has always had a certain... affection for you. Even as thick as he is, he senses that you probably wouldn't consent to... carnal acts." John always chose his words so carefully.

"I don't think the hassle... struggle, really, involved in enacting his fantasies really appeals to him... "

"You mean raping me?"

"Yes. But I don't think he'd be adverse to a situation in which you expressed your opposition less stringently... once you were dead." he finally blurted. "He has some rather twisted tendencies."

"Do tell." I said.

"I'll tell you a story."

"Alright." I said. We continued to walk as he recounted his tale.

"Shortly after you and Timmy left, which was a thoroughly sane decision I must add, though I missed you... I'm digressing.

After you left, the next meal we happened across was a woman. Girl, really, maybe seventeen. She was in pretty sorry shape when we found her; it was a miracle she was alive at all. Well, in Ray's hands, she didn't remain alive for long. So we set her down in the hut, and Con and I went to gather some wood. I forgot something, an axe maybe, I don't know... anyway, I went back inside, and there Ray was, hunched over her, having his way, as it were."

"And she was dead?" I broke in.

"Yes, quite dead."

"Why didn't he just jerk off? That seems like a decidedly less grotesque way to reach the same outcome..."

"I would agree with you, but Ray defies sense. Anyway, I just stood in the doorway, aghast.

146

Eventually Con came in, I guess he was wondering what was taking me so long. He was more vocal. He got Ray's attention, shouting, "Hey! What do you think you're doing?" Well, Ray didn't even look up; he just said 'What? It's not like she knows the difference', which I'm sure was true, since she didn't have a fucking head."

It was the first time I'd ever heard John say "fuck." I turned around and looked at him. He looked red and flustered relating the story.

"... he kept on pumping away. Con was mad as a hatter. He shouted, 'Hey, man, I have to eat that!' and tried to push Ray off of her..."

His voice had trailed off. "What happened then?" I asked.

"I went for a walk." he said.

The silence resumed.

"How much further?" I asked.

"At least a mile."

More silence ensued.

"Hey, John, you really haven't shed *any* blood?"

"Not a drop. The others always did it. I had a good sense for where to find food, and they always took it from there."

"Not even a zombie then? You never got cornered alone by a zombie?" I was shocked.

"I'm a fast runner," he said matter-of-factly.

"So, how are you going to manage on your own?" I asked him.

A thought dawned upon me as I said it. Instantaneously, rage surged inside of me. I spun around.

"You just wanted me around to do the killing for you, didn't you!" I screamed. "To be your fucking hired gun, so you could keep your dainty little hands spotless!" I could barely restrain myself from charging at him. I wanted to punch him, to take this entire, horrible world out on him.

I stifled the impulse. Fuming, I stared down at the ground below me, unwilling to even look at him.

He stopped walking. "No! NO! Adrienne, it isn't like that!"

I lifted my eyes. When they came to rest upon him, my fury deserted me. Looking at him, I realized that I'd never seen him before for what he was—just a pathetic human being struggling to survive, relying on the belief system that he thought could best sustain him. Just like me. Just like anybody.

At that moment, I felt sorry. We exchanged a lingering look; maybe it was a look of regret. There was a lot that could never be said.

I left John standing there in the landscape of rubbish and hurried on. I never saw him again.

Chapter 27

The men had not changed the location of their camp. When I arrived in the courtyard, no one was about. I headed straight into the shack, which had never really served as anything more than a kitchen.

What lay inside left me cold and dead inside. Timmy, or parts of Timmy, were stretched across the scaffold. His upper torso was still intact. There was so much blood. Tears streamed down my cheeks; I could hardly see. I didn't want to see. I remember wanting to hold him, to stroke his hair and kiss his little face, but I couldn't find his head. I searched the floor, through blood, sinews, bones...

When I finally gave up searching, I just hugged myself tightly and rocked on my heels, moaning softly.

Despite my delirium, I was still somehow keenly alert. When I heard footsteps approach, I steadied myself, and waited.

It had evidently not occurred to Con or Ray that I might pursue them. Con walked straight into my wrath. He was very surprised to see me. He came in humming, with a jar of some type of spice in his hands. Holding a gun against his forehead, I noticed that my hands were trembling. They were bloody.

"Child murderer!" I snarled.

"Hey, don't get hysterical. Ray killed him. I'm just the cook." he said.

"I want you to answer one question for me, Con—why would anyone want to eat a child?"

"Well," he said, squirming uncomfortably, "the meat *is* awfully tender..."

"Mmmhmm." I nodded. I had gone quite mad, and I was glad.

"But I didn't kill him... "he reiterated.

"You're all about external locus of control, aren't you, Con? You know, I don't even care if you take responsibility... I'm tired."

I pulled the trigger.

"Shadows on the wall," I mumbled. "Shadows on the wall."

I exited their cave; I was going "huntin'."

Part 4: Nothing Can Stop Me

"Nothing can stop me now, 'cuz I don't care anymore..."

—"Piggy," Nine Inch Nails

Chapter 28

It didn't take me long to find him. He was just outside of camp, lounging in the sun.

"Hello, Ray." I said, pulling back the hammer of the revolver in my hands.

He looked up. "Didn't expect to see you, Adrienne. How've things been?"

"Oh, very good. Very good, indeed. Peachy." I was jabbering and bobbing my head madly, like the maniac I had become.

"Look, about that boy... " he said, sitting up. It seemed to be slowly sinking in that I was aiming a gun at his head.

"Timmy."

"Yeah, Timmy. The thing is, you know he was sick... " He was fumbling for the gun in his belt.

I drew closer to him and pressed the barrel of my gun hard into his forehead.

"Make a move and our conversation ends now." I said coldly.

His arms went slack. I reached down and withdrew his weapon, tucking it into the front of my own dungarees.

"He was dead when we found him, I swear it..."

"You know what I hate, Ray?"

"Ummm..."

"Shut up. It was a rhetorical question. I'm going to tell you what I hate."

He waited.

"I hate bad liars. If you're going to lie, at least have the decency to make it moderately believable... and if you're too stupid to manage that... DON'T LIE!" I leaned down and shouted the last part into his ear.

He clasped his hand to his ear and hunched his shoulders, shrinking from my voice.

"You know what else I hate?"

He waited.

"YOU! I hate YOU, you neo-Nazi nitwit! You stupid, necrophiliac, Ed Gein motherfucker! You goddamned amoral sack of shit!"

"Ok." he said quietly.

I took in a long breath. "Oh, and Ray, there's one other thing I really despise... I mean REALLY detest. You know what that is?"

He waited. When I didn't say anything, he ventured, "What?"

"Oddly," I said, my voice growing low, "I hate finding the one person I love, in pieces, strewn around a room. I find that to be a real bummer."

He nodded.

"I'm done now," I said. "Get on your knees."

I think he begged. I know he whimpered. Honestly, I wasn't paying attention. I shot him, execution-style.

Chapter 29

Acting upon some spontaneous, visceral urge, I cut his organs out. I wrapped them up in his clothing and took them with me to the country, where I lived on them and waited impassively for spring.

That's when the dreams of the rats began. While I was sleeping, those dirty, infectious little creatures would come, in packs, congregating around my head, eating my scalp even as I tried to beat them off of me. They would leave me hairless and bleeding as I scrambled away. Sometimes, before I could retreat, they would consume so much of my connective tissue that I was forced to hold my face up with my hands just so that my flesh didn't slide down and suffocate me.

The dreams of rats weren't so bad, though. They were better than the ones of Timmy.

Chapter 30

Without Timmy, I was empty inside. My love for Timmy had kept me human, and taking care of him had given me reason to keep going. With no innocence left in this world to shelter, no goodness to preserve, nobody to protect, what reason was there for me to keep myself alive?

I became abysmally apathetic. I decided that bad things did, indeed, happen to good people, that the wheel of karma was fucked, and that I no longer cared.

I never returned to the city. The seasons each ran their course, and I lived off of the earth.

Isolated there, I retreated into a vengeful fantasy world, immersing myself in perverse imaginings. In my mind, I began to take delight in playing out how

159

all the people I had ever detested (both acquaintances and public figures alike) had met their undoubtedly unhappy ends. I developed a munificent repertoire of sadistic, zombie-inflicted demises, from which I doled out punishments unsparingly to the unwary victims in the world of my mind. Though withdrawing into a dream world is, admittedly, a pathetic way to deal with unpleasant events, I must confess that I took comfort in it. It was cathartic to kill Michael Douglas and his ilk in the abstract.

Self-important actors were by far not the only ones to suffer my ire. When I had exhausted the entertainment industry and political figures, I turned to academia. I imagined the conversations of all the self-important bastards that populate college campuses and their surrounding coffee houses that must have ensued after the zombies arrived. It was great fun to retreat into my fantasy world and imagine whole philosophy departments analyzing the zombie problem. An endless series of ludicrous scenarios ran through my head. I imagined a dour professor, stating, "Well, you know, zombies can't be real, theoretically speaking... argh! Gargle!" As one fell by the wayside, ravaged by the undead, another would take his place. "...it's an insupportable hypothesis, you see. While a qualia-free replica is, philosophically... Blaargh!" The next one in the line would take up the slack, "Conscious inessentialism dictates... oh, my god! Help!"

Yes, I was bitter, as well as at least marginally delusional. I had lost everything good, so solace could only be found in relishing the demise of all the things I had hated.

Part 5: Gonna Try for the Kingdom,
If I Can...

"...and I,

gonna try,

to nullify my life..."

—"Heroin," the Velvet Underground

Chapter 31

Perhaps I should have been more industrious, stored for winter. But I didn't have the vigor necessary to prepare.

So the winter, this past winter—my last winter—came. I found a cottage to reside in. The house was fairly untarnished when I found it, although my despondent presence has since fouled it.

The residence was so antiquated that it still possessed a typewriter. It was a fortunate thing, since utilities were a thing of the past; any leftover power had dried up long ago. I was done living, so I began to write.

With my writing to occupy me, I pushed my current concerns, my hunger, into a dusty corner. I still had a few of the CDs Timmy and I had plundered; using recycled batteries, I played them again and again. Creating a morbid soundtrack to accompany my miserable life story, I sang along, and kept time with the clack-clack of my typewriter.

But I could not keep it out of my mind; my resolution to starve did not hold.

My skin grew flaky from the cold, exacerbated by my own lack of bathing (I did not have the motivation to go to the stream that winter, as I had done in the past.). At first I merely chewed at my lips and picked at my arms unconsciously while I worked, dropping the flakes from my limbs beside me on the desk after I peeled away each piece. I left the pile on my desk merely out of apathy and disdain for cleaning.

When I finally noticed, after days of absent-minded picking, that I had amassed a substantial pile of dead dermis, it occurred to me that it was *flesh*. I immediately gobbled down that mound of skin, and soon I began to pick away the dry layers of my flesh greedily, leaving countless scabs. I bit at my lips viciously, leaving raw scabs that continually cracked, allowing me to steadily suck at them, nursing from them as if they were a morbid, built-in pacifier. The nervous habit I had acquired of biting the skin around the nails of my fingers also grew out of control; I bit at the flesh daily until I drew blood from all corners.

Unfortunately, these wee meals only served to awaken or, more accurately, to enrage my hunger. As my shriveled belly grew tumescent, the hunger took me. Self-cannibalism asserted itself in my mind as a viable solution. I justified it to myself, pompously saying I needed to fuel myself long enough to finish my story. And so I started with a pinky.

Cutting off my little finger proved more difficult than I had imagined. My hand seemed to have a will of its own, jumping away every time I began to lower the knife.

Finally, I gained the mental control and severed it. It was difficult to stop the bleeding; I applied pressure until I got the flow down to a slow ooze. Then I prepared dinner.

Lopping my finger off wasn't actually as unpleasant as eating it was. Though separated from my hand, it seemed to maintain some sort of psychic link. Every time I took a bite, pain shot through a ghost finger where the digit had been.

A finger is a small meal, really, so I became ravenous again within a few days. I amputated the pinky on my right hand as I had the left.

Typing was becoming difficult. I couldn't really spare any more fingers.

I turned to my toes for sustenance. They were smaller so, except for the big toe, it took two dactyls to make an adequate meal. I ate infrequently, so as to make them last.

I ran out of toes. Shortly before spring reared its head, when my swollen stumps could yield nothing more, I resorted to consuming an earlobe. My memories of it are vague; I only remember undergoing the frustrating, laborious process of removing the many earings from it, grumbling something about ritual mutilations to myself.

When spring came, I alternated between hobbling and crawling to reach the garden; I continued to eat infrequently, due to the bother locomotion had become.

Eating my appendages certainly did not come without a price. The stilted typing and the physical debilitation were inconvenient. And then there was the rotting; it really smelled awful, and I was getting rather sick of inhaling the fruit-flies that swarmed, in a fine mist, around me. Many of my wounds had gone gangrenous, and I had to repeatedly remove moist, atrophied flesh from them. That was plainly an unpalatable nuisance. What was really driving me insane, however, was the itching.

Every digit I had removed had left a ghost in its place, each of which itched like crazy, and I, of course, was unable to alleviate it. How does one scratch an imaginary itch? My miserable, misfiring neurons were torturing me!

Chapter 32

I've been festering for a long time. When I first realized I was dying, I thought about killing myself, sticking a gun in my mouth and ensuring my body wouldn't get up and mill about after I was gone. But I decided against it. I decided to accept becoming a zombie.

I don't believe zombies are evil; they merely exist in a state of id. They have a hunger, so they satiate it. That doesn't seem any more evil to me than our own hungers. In fact, zombiehood almost seems a zen-like state to me now, free from rationalizations and justifications...

I've spent my whole life explaining my environment to myself, trying to assimilate new, inexplicable experiences into my schema. Over and over, I've reshaped my reality, innumerable times, so as to make this world make sense to me. I think that's the curse of the being human; we're control freaks. We can't let things be. The world has to make sense to us, so we obsessively label and categorize. When things don't neatly fit into a niche, we go through the tumultuous process of twisting our perceptions around, until we are able to construct some skewed view that we tell ourselves makes sense. We create order to explain chaos.

Human beings clamber, like fools, to make sense of a multitude of inconsistencies. It's tiresome. I've been confined within my own head for too long. I would like to be able to just accept things, without placing arbitrary judgments or fabricating meaning. I think I shall embrace becoming a zombie as a welcome release. Zombies aren't compelled to constantly ascribe some sort of meaning to their existence. Yes, I long to be undead—to achieve that euphoric, Prozac-like state of complacency.

Chapter 33

I will die very soon now. The infection has spread, and I can hardly even get up from this desk to replenish my candles anymore. My metamorphosis—apotheosis—into catatonia awaits. I will burst forth from this cocoon any day.

My immobility has left me with a lot of time on my hands as of late, so I have been thinking a great deal about becoming a zombie. I realize that life is just a blip—a microsecond. Death, on the other hand, is eternity. It's wonderfully consistent. The only drawback to it that I have been able to discern is that, as a living being, I can still write this down. Creation, creativity, belongs to the living alone. But perhaps artistic expression is only vanity, a form of self-indulgence.

Knowing that I haven't long left, I have been hurriedly scrambling to get down all of my thoughts. Why? For whom? Who remains to read it? It amounts to nothing more than meaningless narcissism. So, this is my legacy. My longing to be recognized, to "leave my mark," will be quelled by death. Death will release me from my vanity.

Zombies aren't really any different from us. They eat the flesh of the living, and we eat the flesh of the dead. Fundamentally, we're all just flesh-eaters.

THE END

About the Author

Alisha Adkins is a native of New Orleans and has also lived in Dallas, San Francisco, and Nagasaki Prefecture, Japan. She holds a B.A. in history and a Masters degree in education. Alisha was a secondary English and history teacher for ten years, briefly owned and operated an eBay store that specialized in quirky clothing, and currently works as an educational consultant for a major publishing company. She is also an avid gamer and acts as a forum moderator for a popular online game.

Written in 1998, *Flesh Eaters* was her first work of length. She maintains that writing it was her natural psychological response to teaching middle school.

Novels for upcoming release by Alisha Adkins include *Daydreams of Seppuku, Death: the Travelogues*, and *Unseen Residents*.

Excerpt from Death: the Travelogues

Prologue

The nice thing about death is that it makes all of your problems inconsequential. However, this is primarily because, typically, death means the end of consciousness, and all of the needling little inconveniences that come along with it – obligations, embarrassments, worries over trivial matters...

I seem to have been part of some tiny cosmic glitch – a miniscule hole in the fabric of existence, or maybe a just a hiccup, one random number out of place in the gigantic computer program of life.

I died, but my consciousness failed to turn off. This was rather unpleasant until I figured out that I didn't need my physical body. Being a consciousness trapped in a rotting husk of meat is rather disconcerting. The living are so accustomed to the organic transports that carry them around that they often cannot separate their concepts of self from their own bodies. I was guilty of similar ignorance. It did not occur to me that my body and I were no longer tethered together. I languished in my own putrid, wrecked remains for well over a week before I figured out that I could just get out and walk.

I imagine that you are wondering then, do I have no physical form? Well, yes, and no. Bodies are merely vehicles for transporting people's consciousnesses around. So, I occasionally hitch a ride.

"Possession" is an ugly word; it is laden with negative associations. There is no malice inherent in what I do; I'm just catching a lift. Sometimes I sit in the back seat and enjoy the scenery. Sometimes I drive.

To brazenly mix metaphors, imagine that you ate the same meal every day of your life. Maybe it is a good meal, or maybe it is an unpalatable one. Regardless, it is always the same one. If you suddenly had a chance to try every conceivable dish currently prepared on the planet, wouldn't you jump at the chance? Well, I would.

A single life is myopic; only since death, with a smorgasbord of bodies available to inhabit, have I begun to form a vague conception of human existence.

Bodies are so... limiting. Being confined to one body, imprisoned in a single ambulatory shell, is so depressingly narrow an existence that it makes me feel claustrophobic to even contemplate it. I can't fathom how I ever was able to stand it. No wonder I was unhappy; no wonder, essentially, at least deep down, all living people are.

I want it to be clear that I am not a ghost or a spirit. If my spirit did survive death, I'm sure it's contentedly floating around a forest somewhere, suffusing with nature. Whatever it is doing, if it exists, has nothing to do with me. I was once a person, but now I am merely a consciousness, or simply an entity. What I was in life doesn't matter; I was the sum of my limited experiences. But, still, my aim is not to be unsettling, and the living tend to find comfort in familiarity, so I suppose I should make an attempt to have you "get to know me." I'll start from the beginning.

Excerpt from Unseen Residents

Chapter 1

When a census is taken, only a fraction of the residents of a household are generally counted. There are typically numerous unrepresented populations. Some may live in the shadows, but others live, unseen, in plain sight. They live openly amongst people, unrecognized, remaining just out of focus or in the corner of their visions.

Human beings today tend to believe that they live in an age of logic, free of magic. The vast majority of people don't believe in magic -- and for the few that do believe in some whimsical sense, it is purely theoretical; they relegate their belief to times of the past -- distant ages filled with beautiful princesses, ferocious dragons, and heroic knights. [1]

---

[1] In truth, princesses rarely were beautiful (due, in part, to

But people's perceptions are shaped by their expectations; magic exists all around them, but they have trained themselves very effectively to not notice it. What they don't acknowledge, they don't have to deal with or explain to themselves. So, amidst a teeming world of magical life, humans insist upon remaining determinedly, resolutely oblivious.

For instance, last month Mrs. Sarah Thompson was upset to see a mouse scurry across her bedroom, yet she stubbornly failed to see the house elf riding on its back. When the same house elf was later decapitated in the mouse trap she set out, she was annoyed that her trap had been sprung without catching anything. She reset it, unaware that she was placing fresh cheese directly into the grisly remains of the hapless elf, and unconsciously wiped the gore from her fingers.

In spite of the death of this elf, known as Buford, (who, tragically, had always been a bit

___

inbreeding), many dragons were quite congenial, and knights, like most other human beings, were generally most preoccupied with their own well-beings.

more dim and clumsy than average), magical beings on the whole are a very adaptive lot. When forests began to disappear around the world, those that lost their homes did not die out; they just moved indoors. However, although far from extinct, they have been marginalized. Across the world, households are rife with disenfranchised magical inhabitants.

Chapter 2

It would be an overstatement to say that outrage had spread through the Thompson house elves' community over the death of Buford; more accurately, his death was simply met with sad resignation. Unfortunately, for house elves, life was cheap; there was always an element of uncertainty when one of them roamed the house. At any point, one of them might perish beneath a inopportunely placed foot, or die of asphyxiation from a sudden burst of some carelessly sprayed bug spray, or fall victim to one of Mrs. Thompson's compulsive bouts of cleaning. Many of their brethren had fallen to the pitiless Vacuum Cleaner of Death.

House elves are much smaller than their woodland counterparts. Fully grown adults stand between just 3 to 4 inches in height. During the night, they make their home in walls, typically using insulation for bedding. Living in the dark would be a substantially more difficult proposition for them if Elven poop were not phosphorescent. Strategically placed public "restroom" locations did wonders for lighting their tenements, though very little to reduce the squalor.

On this night, bathed in the dim glow of a nearby fecal heap, the Dorburt Elf clan was gathered for its monthly meeting to discuss current clan issues. After a long debate on who should be assigned sleeping spaces nearest their clan heap, discussion turned to the recent loss of Buford Dorburt.

"It was an accident," Muldra Dorburt opined. "They didn't mean to..."

"Aren't you sick of 'accidents?!'" shouted an idealistic young elf named Tristam. "How long will we keep making excuses for their behavior? "

"Tristam, please calm down." sighed his mother, Olgaa, slightly embarrassed. "Humans are really quite tolerant. We co-exist quite peacefully, really." she said, trying to subdue her upstart son.

"It's not tolerance!" Tristam said forcefully, spurred by his mother's passivity to adopt an even stronger tone of outrage. "We co-exist only because humans pretend that we DON'T exist at all!"

"Buford really should have known better than to traverse the mean streets of the kitchen."[2] Murdlemem Dorburt, a rather matronly elf in a faded flowered house dress and curlers, intoned.

"Oh, sure, let's blame the victim!" Tristam shot back.

A murmuring of agreement began to run through the crowd.

Emboldened by their support, Tristam pressed on with mounting vigor.

"And Goblin Haaa'chooo *should have known* not to stand where a toy fire engine was going to suddenly, randomly fall from the sky and crack his skull open!"[3]

---

[2] In modern times, many Elven dialects have become permeated with phrases from television.

[3] When Mrs. Thompson cleaned, she tended to lob large objects across the room into piles. If someone was standing in the spot where the first item was to fall, it generally meant that it was curtains for that poor, unfortunate soul.

Again, Tristam saw the crowd nodding.

He began to build toward a crescendo. "And little Burblebutt *should have known* not to play in the tub at bath-time!"

"Well, actually, he really should have..." several elves began to say to one another, looking doubtful.

Tristam sensed that he was beginning to lose them. He needed to end his point swiftly and on a powerful note.

"And," he enunciated, his voice rising, "Troll Splatttt *should have known* that Mrs. Thompson would suddenly decide to throw away the hat box he had been living in (in albeit an extremely cramped fashion) for nearly a decade! Of course, *he had it coming* when the garbage truck compacted him into a foul-smelling pulpy liquid!!"[4]

---

[4] It was common knowledge that the garbage truck had compacted Splatttt into an extremely odorous pulpy liquid because much of him had run out of the sides of the truck and spilled into the street. The Thompsons had tracked this substance inside on their shoes. Its smell lingered in the carpets even now.

Many of the elves nodded vigorously in agreement.

"Well," Great Father Purxxxix, the elder of the clan, said purposefully. His voice was deep and gravelly and his manner of speaking slow and deliberate. The idle chit-chat of the crowd immediately died away as the two and a half dozen elves that made up the Dorburt clan all paused to listen.

"Well," he said again, "the situation is not ideal. We have lived at the mercy of the Thompsons for several generations now.[5] But the fact of the matter..." Great Father Purxxxix paused for dramatic effect. There were perks to being the oldest, and at least perceived therefore as the wisest, member of a clan, and having other elves hanging on his words was one that he particularly enjoyed.

"...is that we can't do anything about it."

The little crowd murmured "Ah." and nodded solemnly. The matter closed, and with no

---

[5] Elf life-spans are considerably shorter than those of humans. The upside to this, at least for female elves, is that elf pregnancies only last three weeks.

other new business to discuss, the meeting drew to an end.

Tristam Dorburt returned to his nest of insulation irate. He kicked at the pink substance, pulled some bits of fiberglass angrily from his tiny boot, and sat down to think.